THE HOLLYWOOD H.I.P.* LIST

The Top 100 lame and laughable scenes in
Movieland that cling to cinematic life like a
big-screen bad guy who just won't die!

DAN MURPHY

THE HOLLYWOOD H.I.P.* LIST
THE TOP 100 LAME AND LAUGHABLE SCENES IN MOVIELAND THAT CLING TO CINEMATIC LIFE LIKE A BIG-SCREEN BAD GUY WHO JUST WON'T DIE!

iUniverse books may be ordered through booksellers or by contacting:

iUniverse
1663 Liberty Drive
Bloomington, IN 47403
www.iuniverse.com
844-349-9409

ISBN: 978-1-6632-2060-8 (sc)
ISBN: 978-1-6632-2061-5 (e)

Print information available on the last page.

iUniverse rev. date: 05/13/2021

AUTHOR'S ACKNOWLEDGEMENTS

No author survives the often-tedious challenge of developing a concept, creating an outline and ultimately writing a book about anything without a lot of support and encouragement.

In my case, I had family and friends egging me on — who *doesn't* like making fun of the implausible scenes that occur in virtually every movie ever filmed? — including my wife Sharon, my brother Kevin, my son Ian and my daughters Fawn and Serena, staunch Murphy Family members all.

But I need to offer a special shout out to my sister Sheila, who shares my love of James Bond movies (and you probably recognized the homage to 007 throughout the book), and to my younger son Brendan.

That's because I "focus-tested" with Brendan dozens of scenarios that I planned to include in the book as we watched many, many Hollywood blockbusters together, and the ones that fell flat I quietly deleted from my list. Nothing like a teen-ager to give it to you straight up and unfiltered.

Finally, my thanks to everyone who previewed various items in my initial drafts. Your thumbs up/ thumbs down responses were greatly appreciated.

— Everett, Washington, May 2021

INTRODUCTION

Considered collectively, movies are arguably the most influential cultural and entertainment medium in the history of the planet — and inarguably the one American export still in high demand around the world.

The best films create larger-than life characters and dramatic scenarios unlikely to occur elsewhere in life. They stir up poignant emotions, taking moviegoers along journeys through worlds created by some of the most gifted storytellers who ever looked through the lens of a camera or had the privilege to sit in a director's chair — inexplicably a cheap folding model with a canvas seat that has their name stenciled on the back.

But although "moving pictures" have been thrilling audiences for more than a century, the craft of filmmaking has changed dramatically in just the last few decades.

Thanks to an army of technical gurus and software programmers using the latest digital imagery tools, contemporary cinema is becoming ever more visually sophisticated. The emergence of high-tech CGI and an endless roster of 3-D imagery have transformed the visuals that animate even the lowest of low-budget moviemaking.

And if the triple-digit tab you shelled out to take the family to the local cineplex was for admission to a knock-off sequel featuring some comic book hero brought to life on the big screen? Brace yourself for two-plus hours of over-the-top special effects and a 120-decibel sound track as entire civilizations get destroyed during the endless fight scenes.

If you need further proof of just how much technology has overtaken the artistry of moviemaking, stick around to watch the final credits of virtually any Hollywood feature produced in the last 10 years. (C'mon. You'll be treated to the replay of a pop song you've already heard a hundred times, which you can then purchase to enjoy as the centerpiece of a downloadable soundtrack album).

As the credits roll following the listing of the hotshot superstars earning millions for their deathless portrayals of fictional superheroes, larger-than-life criminal types or air-brushed historical figures, you'll sit through a seriously lengthy and totally boring list of people you never heard of: associate producers, assistant directors, still photographers, costume designers, camera operators, gaffers, grips, best boys and sound engineers — including, of course, special mention of such luminaries as Animation Effects Coordinator or Head Imaging Technician (and of course "Mr. DiCaprio's Personal Assistant" or "Ms. Witherspoon's Lead Make-up Artist").

Following that, there will be literally hundreds upon hundreds of names listed as digital animators, interactive video compositors, visual effects creators, plus an army of programmers, technicians and post-production special effects personnel.

To make a modern movie, it doesn't take a village, it takes an entire continent.

(And most movies these days are filmed on continents other than North America — thanks, studio accountants looking to squeeze the costs of hiring cast and crew).

Not only that, but a newer generation of screenwriters (allegedly) steeped in the gritty authenticity of the "Real World" are now scripting 21st century films that are meant to be more believable, more reflective of life as we actually experience it, more attuned to the nuance and complexity of our modern lifestyles.

At least that's the premise underlying contemporary filmmaking: No more airy comedies with a cheery-but-clueless family of characters. No more sanitized versions of "based-on-true-events" stories that are more fantasy than factual. And no more phony showdowns between gangsters or gunslingers where the combatants are all firing blanks and even though the scene ends up with multiple actors lying dead in the street, not a drop of blood is visible anywhere.

Now, that's not to say that certain big-screen scenarios don't have a timeless quality about them.

For instance: A guy getting smacked in the privates by a golf ball, a girlfriend or a gorilla is and always will be a proven source of hilarity.

Thankfully, that's never gonna change.

However, the operative word, indeed, the overriding mission in modern filmmaking is "realism."

Family dynamics and interpersonal relationships are raw with angst and conflict. Plot summaries for dramatic storylines reflect searing scenes of pain, loss and defeat.

And the emergence of all those incredibly realistic special effects means that the action / adventure genre now features fistfights, gun battles and combat scenes that are over-the-top gory, graphic and drenched with more blood than a surgical theater during a heart-lung transplant.

It's all about capturing a slice of the Real World, baby.

Yet despite all of this so-called progress, a lengthy list of lame and laughable scenes in Movieland cling to cinematic life with all the tenacity of a big-screen bad guy *who just won't die!*

These are the scenes that either make you groan audibly or laugh out loud. And you'll know 'em when you see 'em, because the geniuses running the industry's leading studios just can't seem to wean themselves off the visual clichés and predictable dialogue that have been staples of filmmaking since the invention of talkies.

PRESENTING: THE DEFINITIVE LIST OF HOLLYWOOD'S

Most Implausible
Yet Totally Predictable Movie Scenes

We'll count 'em down from 100, concluding with a special Top Twenty Ultra-Predictable Scenes — the best of the worst, so to speak.

If you've spent more than a couple hours inside a theater or in front of your TV anytime in the last decade or so, you'll recognize them in less time than it takes to sit through any one of the dozens of ads, trailers and promotional messages that occupy the first 30 minutes of screen time after the theater goes dark.

Kind of like having to wade through this Introduction before getting to the actual content of the book.

What can I say? Here we go. Enjoy the ride.

— **Dan Murphy,** *Everett, Wash., February 2021*

100

The Bulletproof Couch

For starters, here's a classic scene captured on film more times than even the most dedicated cinephile could ever calculate.

It involves an Edgy Good Guy / Flawed-But-Feisty Hero / Renegade-Who-Later-Reforms who's on the run. Unfortunately, he gets trapped inside a palatial mansion, and before he can grab the girl and exit the premises, a gang of assault weapon-toting thugs surrounds the place.

Like all villains in Movieland, they're cruel, they're ugly and they open fire without warning.

Luckily, there's a handy sofa to duck down behind as the bullets start to fly. Even more fortuitously, the foam cushions appear to have been thoughtfully equipped with two-inch steel plating — you know, the kind they use on battleships to withstand a torpedo attack.

That way, even though the would-be killers fire off several *thousand* rounds from every conceivable angle, all that gets damaged in the onslaught are the walls, the floors, the ceiling, the furniture, the windows, the carpeting, several huge pieces of glass-framed artwork, a floor-to-ceiling glass-shelved liquor cabinet, several glass coffee tables, a pair of glassed-in French doors, an entire wall of porcelain knick-knacks sitting on glass shelves, half a dozen crystal chandeliers and anything else that's breakable within a three-mile radius.

Our heroes, thank God, are able to crawl out the front door, make it safely to their car (unscathed) and speed off, miraculously dodging a hail of bullets that kicks up puffs of dust just inches from the rear tires.

Then, they cap off their narrow escape with some completely lame-o line like, "Well, we won't be going back there any time soon."

No s**t, Sherlock.

99

The Backhoe Burial

Okay, on to a wholesale departure from reality that is nevertheless pretty much obligatory in numerous film genres, everything from horror flicks to gangster movies to the occasional dark comedy.

Here's the scene: Someone needs a grave dug (or a coffin dug up). Although it's the middle of the night and the clueless losers doing the digging are in street clothes and dress shoes, equipped with only a dim flashlight, a single garden shovel and just half an hour before the cops show up, they manage to excavate a trench deep enough to double as a submarine dry dock.

Hell, after only a couple minutes of shoveling, they're down so deep they need a step ladder to get out.

Not only that, but the mountain of dirt they've displaced next to the open grave is nice, clean topsoil that appears to have been deposited by a 10-ton dump truck just moments earlier.

Whoa … ya think??

98

Sex Is a Marathon, Not a Sprint

This never-gets-old slice of Movieland magic is as much a staple of the rom-com / chick-flick experience as snacking your way through an entire tub of grease-soaked popcorn.

Only it lasts a *LOT* longer.

According to the sensibilities of virtually every director who ever roamed a backlot, this sequence is merely the predictable, logical outcome of your typical, standard-issue, boy-meets-girl, boy-comes-on-to-girl, boy-rips-off-girl's-blouse, boy-hoists-girl-onto-handy-kitchen-counter and boy-and-girl-leave-a-trail-of-shorn-clothing-that-would-stretch-from-New-York-to-LA, all of which is a mere prelude to a torrid bedroom scene that starts with the onset of Daylight Savings Time and ends when the clocks "fall back" in synch with our power couple as they flop onto the pillows.

The only thing missing is that clichéd scene from those 1940s flicks showing the hands of a clock spinning wildly as uncounted hours elapse, or maybe the superimposed pages of a calendar flying off one after the other like Hurricane Katrina just hit town.

97

The Funhouse Moviehouse

Doesn't matter whether it's a backwoods shack filled with teen-aged slasher-movie victims, a blue-collar bungalow where a family's trapped by scumbag kidnappers, or a crack den in some rundown tenement where a S.W.A.T. team has to roll up a gang of drug runners: Once the cameras get inside a Movieland dwelling, the place morphs into the *Palais de Versailles*.

There are so many balconies, bedrooms, staircases and hallways for the stalker / killer / bounty hunter to sneak around it would take a Realtor half an hour just to list them. Cripes! Where does Hollywood imagine such houses exist?

Uh, other than where most producers, directors and actors actually live, that is.

95

None Is the Loneliest Number

Here's a cinematic question for the ages: Why is it that even though an action / adventure movie's signature chase scene is taking place on congested city streets in a crowded urban neighborhood, once the dramatic car crash / fiery explosion / sustained shootout is over, the bridge / tunnel / freeway suddenly becomes silent and still?

Within seconds, the decibel level downshifts from heavy metal rock concert to the 18th green at The Masters as the winner's lining up his final putt.

There's no traffic, no horns honking, no profanities being shouted out of open windows — unless it's for purposes of comic relief. What was moments ago a bustling thoroughfare suddenly has less traffic than the surface of the moon.

The dark side of the moon.

Which allows the protagonists to engage in a lengthy conversation about what just happened, what they ought to do next and how they're going to get it done — without any interruption from pesky motorists or pissed-off pedestrians trying to get past their smashed-up, bullet-riddled vehicle.

I mean, urban planners in the Real World would *kill* to know how the film's director managed to empty the entire Brooklyn Bridge of people and cars, 'cause that would be a damn useful trick to roll out during rush hour some day.

I'd advise them as follows: Don't hold your breath waiting for a response.

94

The Magic Keystroke Computer

In this all-too familiar scene, no matter what outrageous command the hotshot detective / CIA operative / four-star general barks out — "And I don't want it tomorrow, or after breakfast, I want it *NOW!!*" — all's it takes is a couple seconds of banging by some geek at a keyboard, and *voila*: There's your answer!

"All right, zoom in on the satellite image of the tattoo on that third terrorist from the left."

[Click-click-click]

"Wow. It says, 'Sunnis rule. Shiites drool!' Who knew?"

"I want you to cross reference all red-haired murder victims for the last 20 years with any expired liquor-license violations."

[Click-click-click]

"Here you go."

"Get me a list of anyone in North America who's ever ordered takeout from a pizza place with connections to Sicilian mobsters."

[Click-click-click]

"It's printing."

Yeah — sure it is.

93

Getting Down and Dirty

If the ridiculously expansive interiors in most Movieland houses — even "modest" middle-class split-levels ostensibly occupied by ordinary working folks — aren't implausible enough, at some point the on screen action shifts to a creepy, dimly lit cellar the size of a Walmart parking lot.

Of course, most of that space is usually occupied by a demonic sacrifice altar or some sideshow shrine to a serial killer's multiple victims, but let's not put the cart in front of the horse: Without five or six acres of basement, you can't really construct a lab capable of manufacturing military-grade bio-weapons, now can you?

92

The Amazing Technicolor® Makeup Job

I'm sure every woman on earth would love to know how Movieland heroines manage to survive getting trapped in a thunderstorm, pulled from a burning building, thrown from a speeding powerboat or hijacked minivan (or both) and being slapped around by the bad guy boss after she spurns a come-on that would be a joke in junior high, and then ... when she hooks up with the hero after a dramatic rescue, her hair, lipstick and makeup look like she just stepped off the set of a Maybelline photo shoot.

Look, I know they "ramp up" the spice levels of hot dogs sold at ballparks – which is why everyone says, "They taste better at the game."

I guess the reason actresses look better in movies must be because of those stainless steel canisters of industrial-strength blush, eye shadow and mascara they keep bolted to the side of the director's trailer inside a big case labeled: "BREAK GLASS TO OPEN DURING SHOOTING OF FINAL REEL."

HAIR CARE COROLLARY: While they're at it, why don't Hollywood studios start selling that Eternal Shine shampoo they keep in stock for the actresses they've got under contract? That way, ordinary women could wash their hair, and even though they subsequently spend several days getting drenched in storms, bashed by giant waves as their sea-going yacht is swamped by a mega-tsunami, then enduring a week on a desert island scrounging for food, when it's time for that romantic close-up, their hairstyles would still look fresh, clean and perfectly coiffed.

I gotta believe there's a market for that product.

91

It's Ready in 30 Seconds, Or It's Free!

Doesn't matter how seedy the business might be — a dingy parts supply warehouse, a grimy auto repair garage or a run-down factory of some sort — when Movieland cops show up demanding to know who was driving a delivery truck 12 years ago on a trip to Swampland, New Jersey, the cigar-chomping slob running the joint only has to wheel around to the battered filing cabinet behind his trash-strewn desk, and in a matter of seconds pulls out a manila folder with the exact document the detectives required.

Here's what I wanna know: Is that guy available to organize *my* files from 12 years ago?

90

The Silent, Silent Majority

In this seemingly ubiquitous scene, it doesn't matter whether it's a crowded restaurant, a jam-packed wedding reception or one of those cubicle farms where people are practically sitting in each other's laps: The stars of the show might as well be trapped inside Maxwell Smart's Cone of Silence.

That's because after an initial Awkward Moment when one of the actors shouts out some soap opera-esque line (like, "Okay, I slept with him. But I didn't enjoy it!"), the crowd simply melts into the background like a giant M&M — after it's placed in your mouth.

Not in your hand.

No gawking. No eavesdropping. No hanging around to hear the rejoinder. Everyone not listed at the top of the credits simply turns away and resumes their meaningless mingling, as if in obedience to some off-screen cop telling them, "Okay, folks. Move along. Nothing to see. Show's over."

Hey, it could happen — if you happen to live in Movieland, that is.

89

Mirror, Mirror on the Wall

Whenever a Movieland film — classic or contemporary — needs to depict a struggling loser who's lost his job, family and any semblance of self-respect; a binging alcoholic in the midst of a lost weekend; or a hardcore hitman who's sunk to the depths of depression (although the carnage he creates continues apace), the scenario is practically axiomatic: he stumbles into the bathroom, runs the faucet for *way* too long — up to a full minute if the director's embracing his/her *avant-garde* Muse — while hacking and coughing / struggling to breathe / staring at the water in the basin colored with blood from an open facial wound.

He then splashes some water onto his haggard face, which hasn't seen a razor in days. But he never dries it ... just lets the H_2O slowly drip off his scarred, hacked-up visage.

Although that lame attempt at sobriety doesn't make a dent in the guy's sorry status, he nevertheless looks up at his reflection in the mirror, which, like the ones in a carnival funhouse, always seems to be "enhanced" to show sunken eyes rimmed in dark circles and more wrinkles than an elephant's nut sack.

But instead of recoiling in horror, the guy leans in closer and stares intently at the mirror, concerned and confused, like he's trying to figure out who's that pitiful wretch in the glass.

Which is the trigger for him to drop his head, mentally assess his sad state and horrific appearance, and grimly resolve to A). begin drinking even more heavily, or B). turn his life around and get back to the business of hunting down the bad guys in order to (justifiably) waste by the boatload.

So how come that tactic never works for Real World alkies and depressed losers?

That's just one of those inscrutable mysteries of life, my friend.

88

A Flappin' Good Choice

There's a select list of iconic artifacts and props with which directors have a serious love affair when it comes to shooting a flashback to olden times — ie, the 1950s — or a full-length period piece, also set in primitive times … you know, when photography required film and TVs lacked remotes.

As in, ancient history.

The visual choices vary, from cop cars with but a single, small blinking dome light on the roof (*as if!*) to the well-groomed husband sitting down to the family dinner table wearing a suit and tie to a closeup of an electric coffeepot busily percolating on the kitchen countertop, usually to the accompaniment of a noisy AM radio announcer in the background.

When one particular such artifact is rolled out, however, you can bet the farm the scene will feature a special audio-visual effect … literally.

I'm referring to the classic 16-mm film projector, which appears in numerous cinematic genres, from syrupy sports biopics, where the coach runs film of the opposing team before the big game to a crime caper flick, where gumshoes are enjoying some licentious home movies recovered from a suspect's Hollywood mansion to the classic black-and-white war movie where a roomful of generals reviews stolen enemy film showing secret invasion plans set to get underway.

In all such situations, the dramatic conclusion of the grainy footage ends as a bunch of meaningless numbers and symbols flash on the portable screen, before going to bright white … and then, as the room falls silent, the reel keeps turning as the film lead continues flapping audibly for an overly long stretch of time.

That's so A). you know the film is finished; B). the final few frames (girl's half-naked body on the bed, Hitler-like tyrant exhorting his commanders, etc.) are dramatically enhanced; and C). because *it's a projector*, not some digital streaming source!

Occasionally, directors try to pull off the same stunt with one of those old-school reel-to-reel tape recorders, but I'm sorry — that just doesn't have the same impact as a film lead that just keeps flapping, and flapping, and flapping …

87

Tickets Are Goin' Fast

The setting: A Movieland middle-school musical, which, although the actors are 11-year-olds, features sets and music as sophisticated as those at a Broadway opening, in stark contrast to the "ambiance" of the dark, unattractive gymnasium where the scene takes place.

Nevertheless, the attendance at such events is strictly SRO — standing room only.

The action onstage is obviously low-level — sixth graders in elf suits signing "Santa Claus Is Coming to Town," for example — but there's nary an empty seat in the house.

Oh, except for the aisle seats right near the front inexplicably reserved for the formerly estranged parents (now happily reunited) / the kindly uncle and plus-one filling in for the inebriated, absent dad / the gaggle of stage moms grimly determined that their starlet-to-be, currently dressed as a singing starfish in the Little Mermaid production underway onstage, will totally outshine all the other kids.

For them, there are always choice seats available, even though they waltz in after Act I's nearly over — which prompts a relieved smile from the adorable tween on stage, who due to the protagonists' perceived absence, was moments earlier sunk into depths of depression usually confined to death-row inmates tucking into their last meal before the imminent lethal injection.

86

Top 'O the Lookout to Ya

In the Real World it might seem challenging to set up a video surveillance station / long-distance listening post / tripod with sniper rifle — complete with all the necessary high-tech electronic equipment — in a perfect location to record a drug deal / eavesdrop on Mafioso enforcers / assassinate a rival bad boy.

But not in Movieland!

All the lead actor needs to do is locate a parking garage where his/her targets will graciously conduct their business right next to the outside railings, ensuring complete visual and auditory accessibility. Then hike up to the top of a building conveniently located right across the street, access the doorway to the roof, which is legally required to be left unlocked 24-7, and set up shop.

Unseen, undisturbed and unable to be spotted by another soul anywhere among the dozen adjacent office towers, apartment buildings or industrial structures that all provide direct lines of sight to the perp's rooftop encampment.

It's basically a perfect place to monitor movements, record conversations and/or gun down some potentially deserving target shown on screen in the crosshairs of an infra-red scope attached to the shooter's high-powered rifle.

Best of all, even in the unlikely situation that some nosy tenant, bored office lackey or surprisingly observant homeless guy notices the would-be stalker / sniper / killer on the roof, no one's the wiser. I mean, why would anyone bother calling 9-1-1 just because some commando is perched on a nearby rooftop aiming a rifle at people?

In Movieland's urban America, the sight of an assassin-for-hire zeroing in on his target, well, that's just a routine street scene, mere background noise in the Big City — nothing for a good citizen to bother getting involved with, that's for sure.

85

Slow 'Er Down, Grandma!

The classic, super-slow motion stair lift — whether going up or down; doesn't matter — always provides a lengthy sight gag that rom-com or dark comedy directors just can't resist working into the script.

I realize that for a (presumably) disabled elderly person, designing a residential stair lift that ascends with the speed of a gondola at a European ski resort probably wouldn't be OSHA-compliant.

But in every such scene ever captured on film featuring a bumbling criminal wanna-be / harried husband-turned drug dealer / hardened hitman who still loves his grandma, the saintly senior citizen glides down from her upstairs bedroom at a pace so unbelievably slow that even the snails out on the front porch are complaining, "Hey, you wanna wrap this take before we get old?"

Of course, clueless grandma's relation is in a *HUGE* hurry, given that the residential burglary / six-figure drug deal / cold-blooded killing in which they're front and center was scheduled to take place 20 minutes ago … *hence the comedy!*

See, 'cause Grandma's chair lift is really, really slow, while the need for speed is urgent. But no one can order her to "Speed up!" because she's so sweet, and because the lift only moves at ½ mile an hour — literally.

Which makes for a hilarious couple minutes of comic relief.

NOT!

84

'I'm Gonna Make You Love Me'

Movieland just can't make a final break from filming what has to be the absolute worst romantic strategy *ever*, even though the tactic is seriously "dated" these days (see what I did there?).

Now, this technique can't even be considered if there aren't some "sparks" happening between guy and girl. But assuming that the Attract-O-Meter needle is pulsing (along with pulsing elsewhere), these scenes depict a guy deciding that the best way to advance the relationship — one that's only a few minutes old, let's stipulate — is to force the girl to kiss him.

Of course, modern movies don't go all the way into physical abuse / punitive lawsuit territory, like those early James Bond flicks, where 007 would just overpower the woman and hold the kiss against her will until she could no longer resist his irresistible charm and finally melted into his arms ... and then flat onto her back on the adjacent king bed / convenient chaise lounge / deserted tropical beach.

Unfortunately, the "If at first she doesn't enjoy the kiss, I'll just keep doing it until she does" approach to intimacy still carries legitimacy in *way* too many of Movieland's romantic encounters.

In the Real World, forcing your date to kiss you is pretty much a deal-breaker, as in "WTF?? That's it! I never want to see or hear from you again, and if you contact me, I'm calling 9-1-1!"

But in Movieland, the woman's initial shock and instinctive resistance to an unannounced, forcible kiss is more like a speed bump in an apartment complex parking lot: Yeah, you should probably slow down, but it's not like it's a stop sign or anything.

83

Alone Again … Naturally

In the vast majority of action-adventure-drama flicks, it really doesn't matter if the setting is a two-lane highway running through a dusty desert landscape; a twisting mountain road winding among snow-capped peaks; or even a major thoroughfare in the heart of a commercially zoned urban neighborhood replete with multiple factories, warehouses and industrial facilities.

When the bad boys in the film need to:

- Run a good guy or gal's getaway car off the road
- Conduct an elaborate, seven-figure drug deal
- Hold a dramatic summit meeting of competing crime-family henchmen

They're able to take care of business without another soul in sight.

No cars, no trucks, no traffic. No pedestrians, no police, no people — *period*.

For miles in either direction … nada. It might as well be one of those postcard vistas that portrays the area as if it were a virgin wilderness back in the 17th century or a Google Earth image apparently photographed at 4 am, which depicts nothing but a sea of rooftops on empty buildings.

In the Real World, you try to parallel park your car in front of your house — even in a quiet neighborhood late at night — and six cars drive by within 30 seconds angrily honking their horns and flashing their brights.

But in Movieland, it doesn't matter how long any of the scenes noted above take to unfold, privacy is guaranteed.

Or your dirty money back.

82

The Technical Term Is 'Gouging'

When gunshots ring out in Movieland, the odds are that the dozens of rounds will merely create sound and fury, signifying nothing.

At least in terms of anyone actually getting hit with the gunfire.

But when the script occasionally calls for one of the actors to take a bullet for the director, there's two ways the incident plays out: Bad guy? He either dies on the spot or is merely cropped out of the scene as the action shifts elsewhere.

If it's a good guy character who has additional lines later on in the movie, however, then he'll need to have the wound treated.

Not in a hospital, though, which would ensure proper sterilization and an operation conducted by trained surgeons.

No, the hardcore mercenary / rogue detective / recently un-retired commando instead is transported to a dilapidated truck stop / vacant warehouse / social club doubling as a weapons depot, where a slightly inebriated "healthcare provider" — typically an unscrupulous veterinarian or a medical school dropout — sets to work to treat the injury.

All that's needed is a bottle of rotgut, a hunting knife and an utter lack of empathy for the pain about to be inflicted. The whiskey's divided equally between patient and "doctor," and the knife's is used to dig out the slug from deep in the victim's shoulder or abdomen.

The bullet's then dropped loudly and dramatically into a metal hubcap, the victim lets out a few groans, and *voila!*

The surgery's a success, and after slapping a swatch of gauze over the gaping wound, the hero's good to go. Surprisingly, there are no medical complications, no post-surgical infection and zero need for any rehab before the wounded actor's ready to resume fist fighting, which will inevitably occur later in the movie.

81

An Automotive Mystery for the Ages

Just when Movieland protagonists are all set to head out on a romantic rendezvous / race home to warn their spouse of some imminent danger / execute a harrowing escape from a drug kingpin's hitmen, they regularly face a seemingly preventable but nevertheless problematic complication: their car won't start.

Now, there are two ways this can go.

Option A): The engine turns over, and over, and over, while the actor frantically pumps the accelerator. But it's hopeless, and he/she has to exit the vehicle and try to run away on foot (if it's a woman, of course, she'll invariably trip and fall as her bad boy pursuers are closing in, then lie there helplessly, since getting up and continuing to flee is apparently not possible when you have an extra X chromosome).

Option B): Properly labeled as "The Spielberg Scenario," this option begins with the same initial sequence — the car won't start, the driver grows increasingly frantic, the murderous criminals can be seen in the rearview mirror closing in. But then, with only split seconds to spare, the car suddenly roars to life and the hero speeds off, barely avoiding the fusillade of gunfire that shatters the rear window but inexplicably doesn't injure the driver.

Why not? Look, I shouldn't have to remind you at this point in the book, but those are Magic Movieland® bullets being fired. They're like reverse neutron bombs: capable of destroying all property in sight without harming any human life.

Don't question it; just accept it.

80

A Scripted Sequence to Follow

When the screenplay calls for a scene in which someone suffers a beat down, there's a strict sequence that directors need to follow, proceeding in the order outlined below.

And you can be assured that this is how it works in the Real World, because the current crop of directors have historical precedent as their guide.

What's that? You're wondering what precedent I'm referencing? That's easy: Previous movies from the crime drama, Mafia gangsters and hardcore-street-cops-battling-"urban"-drug-users genres, that's what. Directors know how mobsters, hitmen and other lowlifes wail on someone *because they've watched actors portraying such scenes in other movies!*

Anyway, here's how these potential Oscar clips are typically filmed:

Step 1): The recipient of the imminent beating is cornered and subjected to a quickly escalating confrontation detailing his transgressions — trying to double cross their partner in crime / failing to confess to their ongoing embezzlement of the business where they work / harassing an ex who no longer wants the degenerate to keep contacting their kid.

Step 2): The sucker punch no one ever sees coming. And it's always the classic "Sunday Punch," a wild roundhouse that starts at the puncher's knees and takes several seconds to land square in the face of the victim, who of course is unable to block or dodge the blow.

Step 3): The victim collapses to the floor / pavement / sidewalk, groaning audibly, which prompts the actor administering the beating to roll out another couple paragraphs of dialogue justifying the next step in the process.

Step 4): The kicking begins, and not just a single kick, but multiple kicks, one after the other, delivered not to the victim's head … oh no, that would be way too effective in terms of inflicting pain as punishment. No, the kicks go straight to the midsection of the victim, who's covering up the vital parts down there but nevertheless emits strangled cries of agony with every blow.

Step 5): Finally, the victim lies motionless, which is the cue for the kicking to cease. Satisfied that the recipient has "learned his lesson," the attacker stalks away with one last gesture of contempt — could be spitting on the victim, delivering a final gratuitous kick or uttering one more stinging verbal rebuke, accompanied by an epithet of choice.

Step 6): The camera slowly zooms in for a closeup of the victim, who has (stage) blood dripping from his nose and mouth, plus disheveled clothing and maybe busted glasses. However, after a couple seconds of moaning, he's able to stagger to his feet and limp away, typically recovering enough to resume within the hour whatever activities led to the beating in the first place.

Ain't Movieland great?

79

The Mark of Manly Exertion

How do you know that a Movieland male has been A). Outdoors at 5 am burning up the pavement like an Olympic marathoner; B). Helping a shady brother-in-law clear out some "discount" TVs from his rented storage unit; C). Cooking up a semi-plausible alibi for his spouse that "I was at the gym" to cover for the robbery / beating / multiple murders with which he was involved earlier that day?

Answer: A sweat stain on his t-shirt, always in a nicely patterned "V" running from the collar to mid-sternum.

It looks like some flunky on the set took a glass of water and said, "Hold still," as she carefully poured some on the shirt — not too much, now; just enough to make the "sweating" look natural.

Have any of these people ever actually worked up a sweat from actual exercise? Because if you decide to perform wind sprints for 20 minutes, in South Florida, in July, during the afternoon ... yeah, you will definitely be sweating.

But I'm sorry: your shirt won't have that nice, classic v-shaped stain.

That's reserved for macho Movieland men only.

78

Lights Out? Yeah, Nice Try.

I get why bedroom scenes — other than a steamy sex romp — have to be filmed the way they're universally presented.

But who sleeps with the lights on at night (other than EVERY big-screen character)? Or pretends to fall asleep in a bedroom that's mysteriously lit up enough to capture with perfect clarity whatever action subsequently transpires?

What, is the full moon shining through curtainless windows like it's Go Time for werewolves? Or do movie stars sleep in bedrooms equipped with some "invisible" lighting system that maintains enough illumination so that closeups of the sleeping actors have the same clarity as the test shots used to audition for those very same roles?

Granted, it's annoying during a movie to be subjected to more than a few seconds of a darkened room in pitch blackness where there's only sounds, not sights — unless it's a classic horror flick where a cute coed is about to be stabbed / strangled / slaughtered, of course.

But it's beyond implausible to watch man-and-wife / boy-and-girl characters say goodnight, put away the legal briefs or police files they were reviewing and switch off the matching bedside table lamps ... *but then the room stays lighted!*

Only in Movieland can man truly overcome the darkness, I guess.

77

The Closer We Get, the Deader You Are

Whenever feel-good bonding between formerly disaffected partners, a breakthrough in a troubled relationship or even an outright bromance scene occurs on film, one of the actors experiencing that upbeat, life-changing moment just signed their own cinematic death warrant.

In fact, the happier they are, the more uplifting the scene, the sooner the designated actor's death will occur — and the more gruesome it will be.

For example: Just minutes after the emotionally stunted husband finally confesses to the insecurity that distanced him from his distraught but loving wife, he gets t-boned by a delivery truck running a red light at 50 miles an hour.

Or right after the upbeat scene where the depressed, once-upon-a-time-journalist is motivated by a younger acolyte to finally get cleaned up and resurrect her career of taking down corrupt politicians, she's visited by henchman in the employ of the very bigshot in the muckraker's crosshairs and ... well, the only variable being how the reporter gets snuffed out, coupled with a guarantee that the admirer-turned-would-be partner is the one who discovers the lifeless body just hours after the earlier touching scene.

Or when the formerly despondent schoolteacher questioning his career as it circles the drain suddenly finds out that the kids he thought were defying him were actually inspired by his tough-guy approach and have just posted remarkably positive scores on that all-important standardized test that (for reasons never explained) will determine the fate of the entire school ... well, just hours after the euphoric connection with his students, he receives another revealing piece of information: He's been diagnosed with inoperable brain cancer and has but a week left to live.

Tops.

Unfair, you say? But how else are directors supposed to create that tear-jerking moment in the film, when viewers break out the Kleenex over the fate of some cinematic character portrayed by an actor they don't know, will never meet and who, at the very moment the audience is sobbing in sympathy for his fictional demise is lounging poolside at his multi-million-dollar mansion sorting through potential scripts for his next emotionally touching movie role?

Which he's preparing for by directing his agent to play hardball with the studio and demand that another seven figures be tacked onto his contract.

I mean, how else is he supposed to work up the motivation to pretend to be on the verge of a cinematic death?

76

Glitzy, Gaudy and Gangsterrific!

We've all been exposed to numerous cinematic depictions of a struggling young actor forced to bunk with three frat-rat party boys who relentlessly mock his chances for stardom — which of course is achieved in grand style a half hour later in the film; or the starving artist laboring away in a barren space at the top of a condemned warehouse, whose only amenities are plenty of room for dozens of half-finished canvases and the "luxury" of stretching out at night wrapped in paint-stained dropcloths — only to eventually receive world-wide recognition before the final reel begins for his/her genius-level talents; or the supremely gifted but universally shunned savant laboring away in an unheated attic working toward discovery of some scientific breakthrough — which results in formation of a corporation that builds on that legacy to become a multinational conglomerate, endowing generations of family members with wealth beyond measure.

(*Wow. That was a bit of a run-on sentence, even for me. Sorry about that*).

Point is, Movieland loves to equate poverty and desolate living conditions not only with genius, but ultimately with touching tales of triumph the rest of us can only dream about.

It takes extreme privation to breed such success, so it seems.

There's one glaring exception to that template, however: The headquarters of virtually every drug lord or criminal cabal ever captured on film.

Gaudy isn't descriptive enough to describe how Hollywood imagines the settings where its stable of villainous and totally ruthless kingpins hold court.

Whether a gated compound medieval princes would kill to acquire or some penthouse palace notable for its ultra-high-tech surveillance and security, these dens of corruption always feature lavish furnishings, pricey artwork, super-tricked-out offices, and of course, an overly ornate desk behind which the Big Boss sits while underlings either get issued that day's hit list or who find out that the negative performance review they just received isn't going to result in a demotion but rather in their immediate death.

Turns out that the road to riches isn't paved with poverty but with actual gold, and lots of it.

Who knew?

75

'Here's Lookin' at You, Kid'

It could be a cooking pot in which some culinary-clueless chump is mixing up a gawd-awful concoction; a bank safety deposit box about to be stuffed with stacks of ill-gotten cash; or even a toilet bowl into which the protagonist has just dropped his still-buzzing smartphone.

In every one of those situations, directors must comply with a clause in their contract requiring them to shoot the scene from the perspective of the pot / box / bowl — ie, looking straight up from the bottom of said receptacle to the strained face of the actor staring at what is actually a flat slab of plexiglass.

I mean, you can't really appreciate the stress associated with either hiding laundered drug money inside a secured bank vault or fishing a cellphone out of a urine-laced toilet unless you can witness it from the toilet's or the safe deposit slot's point of view.

For instance: The script calls for the actor to shove a poisoned parcel into a rival gang member's mailbox? We have to see it all happen as if we were hiding right inside the mailbox!

Or he/she has to rummage through a garbage pail to fish out a receipt proving that the crooks bought bomb-making chemicals earlier that day? Thanks to the magic of Movieland, you get to experience the view a trash bin "enjoys" on a daily basis.

It's called Cinematography, and you'd better plan or earning a graduate degree in Film Studies if you have any hopes of truly appreciating the importance of that technique on the audience.

74

If Only Medical Science Had the Cure

In the Real World, a terminal disease is as traumatic as it gets. Family and friends — not to mention the victim — are faced with terrible decisions about prolonging or forestalling medical interventions, while the patient inevitably descends into a state of semi-consciousness, due to the necessity of powerful drugs needed to deal with the pain and suffering that accompanies such situations.

In Movieland, though, there are diseases that not only defy effective medical treatment, but in fact totally baffle the most experienced clinicians: no one can really determine what's going on — but they know for a fact that whatever the heck the doomed actor's afflicted with is absolutely, positively going to be fatal.

Here's the twist, though. Unlike Real World patients, the victim slowly dying on the big screen maintains enough strength to carry on lengthy conversations that pass along entire volumes of acquired wisdom / console other family members in *their* hour of suffering / patch things up with old adversaries who now confess their love for each other in a tearful scene of reconciliation.

Even though the diagnosis is for an imminent, irreversible departure from this mortal coil, the victim of the mysteriously untreatable disease manages to lie there looking a little shopworn but otherwise awfully perky for someone on their deathbed.

Most importantly in such scenes, the end finally comes peacefully, quietly, serenely, as the now-departed actor leaves this life to the backdrop of a soaring orchestral melody, surrounded by a tearful circle of loving friends, family and colleagues.

As tragedies go, the scene is about as upbeat as it's possible to portray — to the point that if a genie suddenly appeared to offer me three wishes, my first one would be, "When the Big Man upstairs calls my number, I wanna go out like a movie star!"

73

Art Is Not Eternal —
But It Is Pervasive

It could be an introverted, socially awkward high school girl sitting silently in the back of the classroom; a love-struck junior partner eyeballing the super-hot female attorney who's the firm's rising star; or just your obviously psychotic loner suspected of being a gruesome serial killer — this scene is almost inevitably connected to all of those characters.

We see them doodling idly on a sketch pad, in a notebook or even on a cocktail napkin. Initially, we can't see what they're drawing, although for most of us it would be some dumb geometric pattern, or a pitiful attempt at sarcasm, like creating 3-D letters that spell out "Boring!" during an overly lengthy business meeting.

But in Movieland, the student's soon-to-be love interest / statuesque fellow attorney / manically dedicated detective tracking the suspect like a bloodhound comes across the paper that was being sketched on and discovers a professionally done portrait of … *themselves!*

Which sets the stage for the student to lift off the geeky girl's glasses and deliver a passionate kiss up against a row of lockers; the bombshell attorney to corner the insecure partner in the hallway and proffer an invite to her swanky townhouse that evening; the cop to throw the paper away and rush home, only to realize the killer's already abducted his wife and daughter, who will survive, bloodied but still alive, as the detective formerly dedicated to "doing it by the book" guns down his adversary in cold blood, rather than even attempt an arrest.

However, the intentional homicide is unanimously endorsed by his fellow cops and heartily cheered by all of us moviegoers, who were not-so-secretly hoping the bad guy would get his head blown off by the end of the film.

Because that's called "justice," don't ya know?

And it all started with some doodling, albeit done by a classically trained sketch artist.

72

Eight Days a Week —
18 Hours a Day

In the Real World, ambitious attorneys-to-be are cautioned while in law school that they need to be prepared for some long hours and their fair share of drudgery on occasion. The legal profession isn't as glamorous as all those cops-and-lawyers dramas portray courtroom dynamics, their professors remind them.

But in Movieland? Whenever there's a high-profile case, the legal team is depicted as working ungodly hours for weeks on end — sorting through box after box after of deposition files; reviewing lengthy transcripts of court proceedings in binders thicker than the Federal Register; and preparing and/ or responding to dozens of motions that have to be buttressed with innumerable citations of relevant case law.

And best of all, they only need several cartons of Chinese takeout a day to sustain them; sleeping, bathing or any other "distraction," like spending time with family members, is not on the agenda.

I'm guessing they had a class in law school on how to order takeout, since there isn't a district attorney's office or a corporate law firm in Movieland that doesn't subsist on restaurant delivery for 99% of the lawyers' meals.

Which are required to be eaten at a conference table while the senior partners / assistant DAs / superhot paralegals debate the merits of whatever case is soaking up that week's 850 billable hours.

71

Will It Ever Come Down?

It's irrelevant which sport is portrayed in Movieland's never-gets-old, heart-warming sports saga genre. Whether we're watching a football, basketball or baseball contest, the final moments of the film defy logic — and gravity — as the pigskin, b-ball or baseball soars through the air for what seems like several minutes.

But *OMG!!* What's going to happen? How will it end? Will the hero complete that touchdown pass as time expires, or sink that last-second basket from *way* downtown, or somehow clear the outfield fence with a four-bagger that wins the game and the girl?

Well, based on a scientific analysis of more than 200 such cinematic epics, I can say with a statistically valid 95% confidence level that the answer is … wait for it … *yes!*

Yes, yes, yes!! The embattled quarterback, whose commitment to the sport and the team were questioned by both coaches and teammates (although not by his super-loyal girlfriend) earlier in the game, comes through in the clutch like a Hall of Famer; or the hotshot gunner who'd abandoned the team the day before the championship game, only to dramatically return late in the second half initiates a scoring spree so scorching hot that the basketball net literally catches on fire; or the slumping, emotionally conflicted slugger who's been embarrassingly whiffed by every pitcher he's faced the previous month finally — with the World Series on the line — crushes a fastball that sends it into an orbit that would trigger a raucous celebration by NASA's Mission Control technicians.

The key to the presentation of these lengthy sojourns in Fantasyland is the long, lingering Slo-Mo shot of the ball floating through the sky — interspersed with half a dozen cutaways of the crowd / teammates / opposing coach wondering in agony what comes next — until it settles in the wideout's arms as he romps into the end zone / kisses the net with a perfect swish / clears the fence as an inebriated fan catches the heroic dinger while hanging onto his tenth cup of beer without spilling a drop.

C'mon. It's Cinema 101. Not that difficult to script.

70

<hr/>

Take Me to Your Leader ...
Or Your Dry Cleaner

No matter how far they've traveled through space, no matter how many light years they've covered since they left their home planet, the alien species who invade the Earth in Movieland always arrive covered with a thick, fresh coat of slime. In fact, I believe the brand they prefer is called UltraSlime®, because it's never too thin, it's never too gooey and it never, ever runs out.

It's UltraSlime!

Of course, your typical aliens are always depicted with supremely ugly "faces" that repulse even bona fide terrestrial monsters, plus horribly deformed limbs and a hideously swollen brain pan with bug eyes the size of dinner plates.

But even though an evil heart filled with

fluorescent green "blood" beats beneath their scaly shells, the thing you wanna avoid the most when you're snuffing out a pod of alien life forms is coming in contact with that icky, sticky slime.

For example: After firing a dozen high-caliber slugs into the protoplasm filling their giant noggins, don't be fooled into thinking they're dead. No, no, no. They're just waiting for you to lean in close to inspect their blow hole — or whatever that pulsing orifice might be — *so they can hit you with a blast of UltraSlime, you idiot!*

Don't do it! Send in an underling buried at the bottom of the credits to handle the inspection. Let *him* get sprayed with flesh-burning slime. Let *him* start screaming as it eats its way through his internal organs. Let *him* collapse into a viscous puddle so the alien can violate him with tentacles capable of piercing the human brain stem, okay?

Dude, in Movieland, that's just plain ol' common sense.

69

World's Worst Employees

Every evil den of iniquity, every criminal hideout, every compound commanded by a corrupt cabal of drug dealers has to be guarded, right? I mean, with mounds of cash the size of the moguls on a ski run sitting around — not to mention a stash of weaponry that a regiment of Army Rangers would salivate over — you can't just rely on a Ring video doorbell as your primary security.

Despite how incredible a deterrent to bad guys that device seems to be on all those TV ads.

No, if you're an El Chapo-class drug lord, a fledgling Third World dictator or even just an ambitious executive whose business happens to be human trafficking or international money laundering you need some serious muscle to protect your operation from other "competitors" in your category.

So why does every Movieland jungle hideout / fortified urban compound / paramilitary training base staffed by ruthless mercenaries universally employ the world's worst sentries? Who hires these clowns? It's pathetic.

I mean, they have only one mission: stand guard and alert the rest of the several hundred armed cutthroats on duty in the event that *anyone* — good, bad or otherwise — shows up uninvited anywhere within 200 yards of the perimeter they're allegedly protecting.

Yet they consistently fail to notice the ninja-like commandos / CIA field agents / rogue military operatives defying orders to stand down hopping over the outer fence, creeping unnoticed alongside strategically placed trees, bushes and/or vehicles and then silently sneaking up and one by one either choking the life out of them or simply delivering the classic cinematic knockout punch that renders someone without a nametag totally unconscious for the rest of the movie.

At some point, you'd think the super-rich, ultra-dedicated masterminds commanding the operation would run a couple Want Ads to recruit guys who actually possess some skills, such as eyesight, hearing and vocal chords.

Because the Movieland sentries guarding whatever strategically situated compound the good guys intend to knock over are uniformly helpless, clueless and worthless.

C'mon, super villains. Get it together to at least even up the odds!

68

A Picture of Perfection

Many parents love to brag about how they're blessed with "the perfect baby," an infant who rarely cries, who sleeps through the night and who hardly ever fusses or whines — even when sitting around in a dirty diaper half the day.

Of course, they're really not being boastful, so much as being relieved that they've somehow been spared from having to confront the trials other parents so graphically describe as they recount their child-rearing experiences.

After hearing too many of those nightmares, the moms and dads who become desperate to avoid the trauma that seems to accompany parenthood now have a solution that's virtually foolproof: Movieland's Rent-A-Baby® boutique.

Concerned that you won't know how to deal with a sobbing infant unable to be soothed? Rent-A-Baby can supply you with a kid who only cries on cue, who loves spending all day plopped in a playpen and who expects no more than a few seconds of affection at a time, lest their cute smiles and happy gurgling distract from the high-priced adults getting paid millions to dominate the on-screen action.

Yes, Rent-A-Baby offers a wide selection of well-mannered infants — as long as you're good with blond Caucasian girls, or a token biracial baby with Caucasian features, only slightly colorized to an attractive shade of mocha.

Oh … that description crossed the line? Really?

Well, how about this dose of reality: The all-too common scene inserted into a plethora of film genres, where an otherwise too-cute-for-comfort infant barfs up on a clueless adult, played either as a comic interlude or as an instructive example of instant karma splashed (literally) onto some baby-loathing adult in the movie.

So, does that balance the scales, get Hollywood off the hook for glamorizing the reality of what's involved in caring for a baby?

Yeah … I didn't think so, either.

67

The Super Macho 'Business' Deal

Granted, a high volume of "recreational" drugs arrives in the USA from countries south of the border. And the residents in most of those points South tend to be of Latin heritage.

But whenever moviemakers want to depict a searingly realistic exchange of ill-gotten cash for dangerous (and illegal) drugs, the participants are all hardcore Hispanic hitmen whose menacing looks — enhanced by plenty of bling and tats — are matched only by their twitchy eagerness to pull out any of the multiple firearms they're packin' and start wasting everyone in sight.

And there's always a serious discrepancy that threatens scuttles the supposedly well-planned deal … one that, in fact, has been so tightly arranged that even the undercover cop who's infiltrated the gang can't figure out the date, time or location of the deal.

Either the buyers are short a couple of the dozens of stacks of machine-wrapped Franklins stuffed into a duffel bag, or else the dealers decide — always at the last second — that they're gonna need way more cash than the already outrageous amount previously agreed on.

Allegedly, the participants are all seriously experienced at conducting these clandestine deals — you and over cash, we hand over drugs — but the transactions always have more unforeseen problems than an Enron audit.

Only instead of subpoenas and arrest warrants, however, the drug dealers' issues are settled with several minutes of gunfire that wipes out everyone who doesn't have a contract to appear in a future film.

In the Real World, most illegal drugs are distributed via legitimate channels of commerce and the money is transferred with the same system we all use: electronic deposits.

To be honest, though? That would make for a really boring movie.

Nobody wants to see John Wick or Jack Reacher standing in line at an ATM waiting to retrieve their deposit slip and pocket a couple hundred dollars in walking around cash.

Hell, that doesn't even make for interesting security cam footage.

66

It's All About the Timing

It could be a crime drama, a spy-versus-spy action flick or even a comedy about bumbling good guys trying to pull off some criminal caper: When a crucial development in the plot needs to be dramatically presented, there's a tried-and-true method that hasn't failed in decades of moviemaking.

Here's how it works:

The strikingly hot legal assistant / nervous spouse / brainy-but-off-putting junior detective hustles into the room or office where the star(s) are holding court and breathlessly announces: "You gotta see this."

Without missing a beat, he/she grabs the handy remote that's sitting right in plain sight (unlike yours or mine) and with one click the television instantly displays a commentator or news anchor right at the beginning of a segment explaining some serious setback or horrific disaster affecting the high-profile lawsuit / crime wave investigation / status of a super-rich couple's kidnapped kid being held for ransom.

As the stunned group of actors watches silently, the talking head flashes a photo of the suspected serial killer / escaped convict / arrogant defense attorney revealing some previously unknown piece of evidence that threatens to scuttle the entire case.

Of course, the classic twist on the convenient introduction of Preternatural TV Timing occurs when a wrongfully accused suspect-on-the-lam / wanted killer attempting to hide his identity / deadbeat drifter who just murdered an entire family is trying to blend in while sitting at the counter of a dingy diner or tavern.

And guess what?

The television set *AGAIN* just happens to be tuned to a news report flashing a mug shot of the guy, which cues the nosy waitress / snarky bartender / off-duty cop chowing down on pie and coffee to case the guilty-looking loser up and down — coupled with a double take: looking at the TV, then back at the guy, then back at the TV — while casually writing down a description / surreptitiously reaching for the phone / suddenly unholstering his handgun, respectively.

Which prompts either an implausible escape, an immediate seizure of hostages, or if it's a Quentin Tarantino film and pretty much everyone in the scene is packing semi-automatic weapons, an over-the-top bloodbath.

Filmed in Slo-Mo.

Of course.

65

The Slowest Car in
Automotive History

Is it possible for the average person to outrun a speeding car?

Hell, yeah — if we're talking about a Movieland scenario, not what would actually occur in the Real World.

Before you scoff at the very premise of that question, remember: The camera not only adds 10 pounds to the actor, it subtracts 10 mph from the vehicle.

Thus, when the hero suddenly realizes that the bad guys have wheeled their car around with the engine revving and the tires squealing, he starts running down the street. But he isn't looking for a narrow alley he can duck into or a telephone pole he might run behind ... oh no. Instead, he "sprints" right down the middle of the road, actually following the center stripe like it was a giant magnet and he's wearing cast iron shoes.

And to make it worse, instead of just putting his head down and sprinting, he continually twists around to look behind him and gauge how fast the car is gaining on him.

So … what happens to the star of the film? Does he end up like some possum that foolishly tried to cross the road?

Do you really need me to answer that?

64

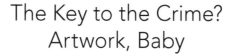

The Key to the Crime?
Artwork, Baby

In order to stop a horrific slew of murders and catch the ultra-evil psycho responsible, you'd probably assume the homicide squad super sleuth / ex-cop-turned-PI-revenger / rogue detective disobeying orders to stand down in the hunt for the deadly serial killer would deploy surveillance tools to track suspects, use online research to explore possible clues or even go to the old-school witness interrogation card.

Wrong.

Instead, the countless hours that roll by as the body count continues to pile up during the first 60 minutes of the film are spent creating the ultimate arts-and-crafts project (which appears to be a prerequisite for anyone in law enforcement to earn their detective's shield): A entire wall of head-and-shoulders shots of seriously nasty-looking suspects — with black marker captions underneath each one — all crisscrossed in inexplicably complex fashion with multiple strings of yarn.

From the looks of it, it seems like the cops spent a couple hundred bucks on yarn alone — not to mention how fortunate it is that the otherwise cramped precinct station has an entire blank office wall available to create the sprawling display.

However, despite the artwork's utter failure to provide any useful context that might identify the killer, the lead actor spends entire shifts during the ongoing crime spree staring hypnotically at the display, expecting, so we're led to believe, that any moment now a sudden inspiration will bring it all into focus and provide the vital insight necessary to catch the previously untouchable perpetrator.

And you know what? It works! No matter how cluttered and confusing the art wall appears, the tactic *always* works!

In Movieland, staring intently at a bunch of photos connected by so many lines of yarn that the spiders in the room have given up trying to compete eventually leads to the breakthrough that every other method of criminal investigation failed to produce.

I mean, it makes sense if you think about it … the way a gifted detective is apparently able to "think" about an inscrutable maze of pictures and string, that is.

And in case you suspected that prior to shooting the scene some production assistant just slapped a raft of mug shots on the wall, randomly connecting them until the yarn ran out, I got a newsflash for you: It's called Forensic Science, my friend … uh, although in Movieland it's kinda more art than science.

[The previous insight was brought to you by your local Hobby Lobby retailer, law enforcement's preferred source for seasonal decor, craft supplies and most importantly, yarn!].

63

Fast-Acting, with Instant Results!

In Movieland, whenever the lead detective / senior partner / business bigshot — basically anyone with any authority whatsoever — mouths the proverbial line, "Give us a minute," the interrogation room / conference area / corporate lobby empties out like someone shouted, "He's got a machine gun!"

It's amazing how compliant everyone else in the scene becomes, although in many cases they've entered the room moments earlier planning to conduct some seriously important business.

In the Real World, someone tries the same tactic and they get an immediate response, as well — only it ranges from "Really?" to "What's going on here?" to "Who the f**k do you think you are?"

But in Movieland, nobody so much as glances sideways at the person issuing the request or expresses even the slightest annoyance at the impromptu evacuation, because in the same vein that Henry Wadsworth Longfellow noted that music is the universal language of mankind, so too is the "Give us minute" comment also universally accepted and understood by whoever's within the sound of the speaker's voice.

Heck, judges sitting on the federal bench don't get the same level of cooperation when they order the courtroom cleared for a recess to confer with the attorneys over some significant point of law.

But in Movieland? The lead actor's wish is everyone else's command.

62

The Steel-Skinned SuperHero

Used to be that the worst physical punishment a movie star had to endure was getting a balsa wood chair smashed over his shoulders in a carefully staged saloon brawl, or taking a fake punch to the chin that actually missed its mark by half a foot.

Of course, contemporary fight scenes have to be seriously jacked up — for the sake of "realism," don't ya know?

So now, moviegoers get to watch their heroes suffering unimaginable punishment, only to pop up, dust themselves off, touch that tiny trickle of blood conveniently restricted to the side of their face and fire off an even more painful comeback line:

- Like getting bashed in the face with a stainless steel bar, then muttering, "Ow. That's gonna leave a mark."

- Like tumbling headfirst down several flights of concrete stairs while locked in a Greco-Roman wrestling hold with an attacker — which snaps the bad guy's neck like dry kindling but leaves the hero with nothing worse than momentary dizziness he quickly shakes off with a snarky comment like, "That first step's a real killer."

- Like getting savagely kicked in the ribs by thugs the size of football lineman, then hopping up and snarling at the ringleader, "Your friends play rough."

- Like getting pushed off a 10-story building, only to land in an open Dumpster that just happened to be filled with bags of discarded foam peanuts, then shrugging as he tells his partner, "I guess some guys have all the luck."

As The Terminator would say: "My sensors register the data. You could call it luck."

Or, you could call it a two-syllable word denoting something else a whole lot more "aromatic."

61

Listen Before You Speak

When the conflicted hero knows that s/he needs to make that all-important phone call to confess their infidelity and/or criminal activities; to reveal where the secret cache of ill-gotten cash is stashed; or to beg for forgiveness, even though they've wrecked their marriage, endangered their children and had to murder half a dozen people to cover their tracks, they dial up the recipient's phone number — always on speed dial; I mean, who's got time to tap a bunch of buttons? — and then with a facial expression usually reserved for prisoners being tortured, they listen to the voicemail greeting.

But they then quickly disconnect before the other person can answer, and certainly before they have to leave a message.

However — the angst and anxiety are too overwhelming, and a few moments later the guilt tripper is forced to redial, only to either repeat the same performance all over again, or to bail by leaving some cryptic message like, "Hey, uh, just checking in."

That's how us moviegoers realize that the actor is *STRUGGLING* to come to grips with his/her conscience, battling the need to come clean with a deep-seated reluctance to truly spill their guts, seeing as how what they've been up to ain't exactly peddling Girl Scout cookies.

'Cause when you're cooking and selling meth, embezzling millions from some business or just killing people straight up for cash money, it's not easy to reveal the "other side" of your personality to loved ones, close friends and of course, law enforcement.

That latter piece is where the aforementioned "angst" originates.

Just so you know …

60

The Invisible Stakeout

Whether it's a Tough Cop / Goofy Buddy pairing, a Break-All-the-Rules-But-Get-the-Bad-Guy detective duo, or even your plain vanilla, second-unit street-cop stakeout scene, the long arm of the law is apparently tougher to spot than Harry Potter's Invisibility Cloak.

That's because whether it's a four-door Crown Vic or a full-sized step van with "Joe's Plumbing" stenciled on the side, the kidnapper / terrorist / serial killer under surveillance always glances up and down the street before entering his hideout in a rundown tenement — only to miss the one suspicious vehicle that looks totally out of place and in fact has two crew-cut FBI agents with earpieces staring at him from behind the windshield.

Hey — it can happen to the best of us.

59

Third World-Class Stereotypes

No matter how small the budget for a straight-to-cable action flick, Central Casting seems to have a never-ending supply of cut-from-the-same-cloth ethnic evildoers.

It's like scanning the *tapas* menu at one of those trendy LA eateries: Would you like heartless Latino drug thugs, sadistic African warlords, fanatical Arab terrorists, craven ex-Soviet super spies or greedy Asian crime bosses? Or maybe the combo plate, where you get a sampling of all five?

Doesn't matter what the plot might be, or how thin its relationship to the string of explosions, shootings and car chases crammed into pretty much every scene, moviegoers can be assured of one eternal certainty whenever they sit down to a Hollywood blockbuster: You can always tell the bad guys — even without a scorecard (or a soundtrack) — simply by waiting for the senseless, cold-blooded mayhem that's sure to follow even a few seconds of screen time for any of these non-white, non-photogenic, nonsensical villains.

58

The Hapless Henchmen

In addition to their evil DNA, there's one other constant for Movieland's Bad Boy Bosses: They always seem to be surrounded by a boatload of suicidal hangers-on *way* too eager to get themselves gunned down, beat up or blown apart as the good-guy commandos / one-man mercenary / S.W.A.T. team battalion storms their secret compound.

Whether they're sprinting heedlessly into concentrated machine-gun fire, rushing single-file (one at a time, please) at the karate-kicking male lead — only to get a combat boot in the face for their efforts — or jumping in front of a two-ton truck for the privilege of becoming body No. 327 to be sent flying through the air to a grisly landing on a pile of sharpened, scrap-iron bridge railings, these brain-dead losers apparently have no motivation in life other than seeing how fast they can get themselves snuffed out in whatever hopeless scenario some second-unit director dreamed up.

Hey, it ain't great, but it's a living.

So to speak.

57

The Last Sap Standing

But the most ridiculous of the Hapless Henchmen is the action flick's quintessential stooge. Here's how his "moment of glory" inevitably plays out:

The scene begins when a gang of thugs ambushes the hero in a sleazy pool room or maybe some generic urban storefront. In any case, there are two key elements: Overwhelming 20-to-1 odds against the good guy, and lots and lots and lots of breakable furniture, glassware, shelving, tables, chairs, pool cues, bottles, dishes, windows, etc.

Of course, the would-be killers have better manners than Emily Post, politely taking their turns attacking — not by firing any of the three dozen automatic weapons they're packing, mind you, but instead by bull-rushing the hero with club or knife attacks that are so blatantly telegraphed they might as well just announce them over the PA system on the set right as they're happening:

"Your attention, moviegoers. Introducing next, attacking from the left side of your screen: Vinnie 'The Animal' Barbosa. He hails from Upper Cesspool, New Jersey, and boasts an enviable record of 74 shakedowns, including 27 fatalities, with only two criminal convictions. He'll be swinging a large steel chain, which will prove surprisingly easy for our hero to dodge, rip out of his hands and then bash in his head with the same move Vinnie tried just a second earlier. So ... let's get ready to rumble!!"

After several minutes of bone-crunching kicks, skull-shattering head butts and neck-snapping kung fu strikes — all accompanied by the explosive destruction of the entire soundstage — there's only one bloodied, punch-drunk bad boy left. His arm is dangling by a thread, his teeth are somewhere strewn around the floor, and he's limping *badly*, probably because his right femur was shattered by a blow from the very baseball bat he was using to attack the hero moments ago.

So should he make for the exit? Live to fight another day?

Oh, no. Instead, the snarling gang leader (who stayed safely out of reach) issues an order to "Get him!"

True to The Oath of the Hapless Henchman, the sap staggers forward, propelled by a completely inappropriate battle cry, only to succumb seconds later to a scene-stealing, ultra-gory demise, after which the hero wrenches his still-beating heart out of his chest and holds it up to the bad-guy boss while whispering some immortal line like, "He won't be needing this anymore."

No, I guess he won't.

56

Welcome to the Dark Ages

Directors who specialize in the cinema, who are ultra-hip, super-smart, with-it guys and gals — I mean, just listen to their Oscar acceptance speeches — love to send "signals" to moviegoers to set the scene and the time period.

Now, some Neanderthals actually run a big bold headline on the screen like, "Los Angeles - 1959."

But a much cooler approach is to use visual cues to hit viewers over the head with the message that *we are now back in the past!*

Here are the three most popular techniques:

1). The Trashy TV. Apparently, television sets manufactured prior to the invention of the flat screen were basically shoddy, unreliable pieces of crap. That's because the black-and-white picture is always plagued by constant, grainy distortion, requiring the irritable dad / perky, know-it-all mom / precocious tween-ager to hop up and start swiveling the rabbit ears antenna — staring at the rest of the family instead of the screen while attempting to remedy the unwatchable blur of static.

Optional: If it's a stressed-out loner or a drunken party boy attempting to watch a program, the failed attempt to jiggle the rabbit ears is then followed by a violent smack to the side of the TV cabinet ... which instantly fixes the problem, leading to the obvious question:

Why not just *start* by whacking the set?

2). The Home Liquor Store. To believe most period pieces set in the '40s or '50s, the typical suburban living room featured a well-stocked liquor stash equipped with enough varieties of spirits to open a boutique barroom. Not only that, but there's always a crystal canister sitting on the sideboard full of ice cubes that never seem to melt.

Best of all, these scenes drive home the reality that was apparently prevalent way back when, and that's the answer to the question: When's a good time for a stiff belt of bourbon?

ANYTIME!

3). That Glamorous Smoky Haze. Okay, plenty of people smoked cigarettes back when they were known as cancer sticks or coffin nails, rather than the modern deterrent of labeling packages with a stern warning from the Surgeon General.

But whether it's a hardcore private eye draining a flask of whiskey, a hotshot businessman hustling clients or even a glamor girl nightclub singer crooning the final notes of her set, virtually every waking moment with every character is spent lighting up, blowing smoke rings or waving a cigarette theatrically to punctuate some snarky conversation.

For movie characters in the mid-20th century, it was axiomatic. Stressed out? Light up. Anxious? Have a smoke. Celebrating? What better way to commemorate the happy event than sucking down some tar and nicotine?

Life just went better with cigarettes back then ... well, until later on when you had to be tethered to an oxygen tank bolted to your motorized wheelchair.

To summarize: When the big screen's filled with more smoke than a forest fire; when the TV reception totally sucks; and when swilling hard liquor takes the place of eating meals, that's how you know the action is back in the past.

55

You CAN Get There from Here

In this obligatory scene for a drama or action flick, the normal constraints of time — and certainly space — are fully suspended.

That's because while it would take ordinary humans hours to travel across town, much less to another city altogether, in Movieland, that journey requires mere moments.

It doesn't matter if you're a 10-year-old on a one-speed bike or a teen-ager on foot — distance is all relative on the big screen; the miles just fly by like you're Peter Pan and you really believe you can fly!

For example: When the hero needs to show up at the hostage scene just in time to gun down the bad guy seconds before he plunges a knife into the swimsuit model lookalike he's holding captive, the director can't let a little inconvenience like the fact that the guy was 20 miles away 10 minutes ago stop him from capturing that final reel grabber.

Or when the seedy ex-detective who got bounced from the force because of the Frank Sinatra Rule ("I Did It *My* Way, Bro!") is hunting down a serial killer, with his only clue a gasping comment ("He's in a red house") he tortured out of some lowlife covering for the psycho, why, he can just pull right up to the exact location in his macho SUV (without provoking any suspicion, of course) in less than 10 seconds of screen time — in the dark, in a strange city and with blood dripping down his face from getting stomped on by street thugs minutes earlier.

The rest of humanity takes half an hour of creep-and-crawl just to find an unfamiliar street, much less locate the house numbers. Our movie star, though, apparently has a GPS chip implanted in his skull, because he never gets lost.

And if he does happen to take a wrong turn, well, he just follows his heroic instincts: Simply wheel your vehicle around 180 degrees in a violent skid and proceed to drive at high speed in the opposite direction. Onto the freeway. Against traffic. During rush-hour.

I mean, it's so obvious, I shouldn't even have to mention it.

So a couple dozen cars get totaled. What's your point?

54

The Supersonic Smartphone

For most of us, you drive an hour out into the sticks and your cell service gets downright spotty. Movie studios, however, issue phones to the stars that appear to have been stolen from an alien civilization, because they never go dead, they never lose reception and you can shove one into your coat pocket while a gun-toting villain holds you hostage, and people a continent away can hear both ends of the conversation on speaker phones like you were sitting right next to them at the table.

Oh yeah. Those Hollywood handhelds also filter out unnecessary conversation, which is a nice little plus when you're trying to trim your cinematic spectacular to a tight 90 minutes of run time. No pleasantries, no idle chit chat, no let-me-introduce-myself conversation ever gets through.

The phone rings, the good guy answers — always with a gruff "Yeah"? or "Go!" — and two seconds later, he can stow the phone and announce, "They found the body. Let's move."

Gotta warn you, though: That feature costs extra every month.

53

The Older They Get, the Harsher They Sound

This ubiquitous piece of casting cuts across virtually every movie category. You could be soaking up a family feature, a dramatic adventure film or a straight-to-cable comedy. Doesn't matter: The portrayal of anyone older than 60 is as predictable as cleavage on the red carpet.

Only a lot less entertaining.

First of all, granny or grandpappy's always feisty, short-tempered and highly opinionated — in other words, grumpy, rude and foul-mouthed. They comment caustically about the younger generation — specifically, the family members co-starring in the film — and denounce every modern development since the invention of AM radio.

If you're really lucky, and the director realizes he or she's gotta flesh out a 30-minute sitcom script into a full-length feature, you get treated to a classic "Back in my day … " diatribe that rambles on about life in what starts to sound like the Pleistocene Age.

But underneath the oldster's bluff and bluster lies a heart of gold, plus more wisdom than Solomon and Socrates squared. Only you have to hack through sedimentary layers of bitterness and alienation with a metaphorical jack hammer to get to the goodness that lies inside.

And of course, the apple-cheeked, tween-aged star of the show is the only one capable of finding that goodness amidst the tidal wave of negativity that screenwriters apparently believe animates just about every human being collecting a Social Security check.

It's all so heartwarming, I-I think I'm gonna cry (*sniff*).

"Now get off my lawn, ya whippersnappers! Cut out that tomfoolery or I'll knock some sense into you punks with my cane!!"

52

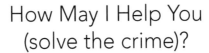

How May I Help You (solve the crime)?

In the Real World: You approach a hotel's front desk, to be greeted by a clueless co-ed whose only response to any communication other than "Hi. My name is _____ and I'm checking in" is, "Um-m-m ... lemme ask my manager."

In Movieland: A pair of detectives approaches the front desk, where the over-dressed, overtly gay clerk at the counter provides more pertinent information in a single conversation than the chief archivist at the New York Library's Reference Desk: Who checked in, when it was, what she was wearing, the guy who accompanied her, the room service order they phoned in and the "approximate" checkout time rounded off to the nearest minute.

All from memory.

Oh, yeah. He also "happened" to overhear the pair talking about catching a cab to the airport. Possibly for an overseas flight. Probably on United Airlines. Leaving at 10:30. Gate D7. Check-in at 9:15. Traffic's bad — better hurry. You're welcome, detectives (wink, smile).

And all's it takes to get this mountain of intel is flashing a badge, plus a veiled threat to "Check out what else is going on behind the counter," and the clerk is squealing like a Mob rat entering the Witness Protection Program.

And half the time, they're still using that completely obsolete "guestbook" they swivel around so the cops can compare the signature of Ms. Good-Girl-Gone-Bad against a letter they (illegally) pilfered from her apartment earlier that evening.

As if!

51

Keeping That Permanent
Pressed Look

Here's your next scene, studly male action hero:

- You just emerged from a half-hour underwater swim through a mine-filled moat and now you're standing on a muddy bank in the dark stripping off your wetsuit.
- Or you parachuted down from a jetliner cruising at 30,000 feet above the conveniently deserted neighborhood park where you just happened to land.
- Or you had to navigate down an Alpine glacier on a stolen snowmobile while bad guys aimed rocket-propelled grenades and shoulder-fired missiles at your fleeing ass.

No matter how perilous your journey, when you step into the posh casino moments later to check out the super-villain you're tailing, your Brioni tuxedo is immaculate — white shirt sparkling, slacks perfectly creased and shoes so shiny "They look like f***in' mirrors."

You're so impeccably outfitted, the mannequins at Neiman Marcus are jealous.

Given the circumstances, how's that even possible (the impeccable part, that is)?

Good question.

50

The Smaller They Are,
the Harder They Hit

Ever been punched in the face?

It hurts like hell, and it's generally followed seconds later by one of two developments: Either you're spouting profanities at a clip that would make a band of pirates start to blush, or you're sitting on your keister (or flat on your back) groggily realizing that not only your pride, but several of your more prominent facial features just got crushed — in which case, the swearing's only slightly less vocal.

In fact, in the entire history of humanity there have only been a couple dozen documented instances where a single punch knocked someone out cold, with no yelling, no moaning and no perceptible movement for the next several minutes.

And fully half of those exceedingly rare occurrences are attributed to one guy: Mike Tyson.

So what are the odds that a 110-lb. starlet, whose most impressive physical assets are bouncing around inside her bra, could pull off a one-punch knockout?

According to Hollywood calculations, about 99.99% of the time.

Now, obviously, it helps amp up the power if the hottie happens to be wearing a skin-tight black leather outfit, or maybe a pair of eight-inch stiletto heels. But even if she's just your run-of-the-mill, dime-a-dozen, supermodel-skinny, looks-great-in-test-shots "discovery" some director's been shagging, in Movieland she can drop a 250-lb. career criminal with a single spinning kick to the head.

And he *stays* dropped, lifeless and still, to be revived only when he hears that magic word: "Cut!"

How does she do it?

Don't ask. Just enjoy.

49

Stereotypes 'R Us

Who's the "It Girl" in contemporary Girl-Gets-the-Guy rom-com role reversal flicks?

Well, she's 20-something, super-ambitious, upwardly mobile and able to handle extraordinary feats of multi-tasking: yakking on the phone to a reluctant supplier as she bargains for a never-before-agreed-to price point, while directing subordinates to prioritize their daily to-do lists with nothing more than active finger-pointing, even as she scans a computer screen displaying a spread sheet that would stump the CEO of H&R Block.

By the way? She's very, very attractive, but moviegoers don't realize it right away because her hair's yanked back in a bun so tight it doubles as a face lift and she has "smart-girl" glasses glued to her nose, even though she has perfect 20-20 vision.

Plus, although she's the CEO of a hot new start-up located in a spacious, upscale office tower, she's attired in outfits so outdated they look like they came off the free rack at a Goodwill store.

She's paired with a "Boy Foil" in such comedies, a handsome, hunky but currently career-challenged love interest who's as unambitious about business success as he is determined to break through her icy exterior and hook up with the It Girl, who of course, totally spurns his advances for the first half of the movie.

Boy Foil dresses down in faded but expertly tailored jeans, deck shoes sans socks and a casually unbuttoned sport shirt that doesn't do much to conceal his exceptionally manly pecs. Typically, he hires on at It Girl's emerging corporate powerhouse as a lowly office boy without any apparent responsibilities, other than making (rejected) moves on the It Girl, while fending off relentless come-ons from every other female in the organization.

Of course, the It Girl also has to brush aside ham-handed invitations for after-work socializing from all of the males she encounters, either in her company's elegant headquarters or out in the business world with clients, colleagues or competitors.

All she has time for during her 14-hour workdays is barking at her harried assistant — who can barely keep up with the nonstop commands issued every couple minutes — to *PLEASE* fetch a triple mocha latte with caramel drizzle and cinnamon sprinkles, which It Girl desperately needs to gear up for that important 9 am meeting with the banker who wants to lavish another $100K in low-cost lending to fatten her already astounding bottom line.

Oh, after all this set-up you were wondering about the plot of the movie? Allow me to summarize:

For most of Act II, Boy Foil ridicules It Girl for her slavish devotion to business success, while she slams him for his misguided love of a life other than work. But then both of them encounter a serious crisis: She needs help to repair a troubled relationship with her once-and-future father-mentor, while he suddenly needs a mountain of cash to (secretly) pay for life-saving surgery needed by his single-parent sister's disabled son.

Solution: Girl volunteers to fork over the money for the surgery, if Boy helps her learn to relate to humans with the same skill she possesses in analyzing balance sheets. They have a heart-to-heart over way too many drinks at some hip neighborhood wine bar, as he asks, "Why are you so driven?" and she counters with "How can you be so carefree?"

The bonding concludes with both agreeing to revamp their lives (although they admit "This is gonna take a lot of work!"), with the unspoken payoff for both of 'em being some serious sack time down the road.

Next day, It Girl strolls into the office decked out in outfit by Prada, shoes by Jimmy Choo and accessories by Louis Vuitton. Shockingly, the glasses are gone, the hair's professionally coiffed and she actually says hello to the dumbfounded staff members who silently watch her waltz by as they stare at her with their mouths wide open.

Moments later, Boy Foil shows up, this time with hair closely cropped, beard neatly trimmed and outfitted in a sharp new sport coat and dress shirt by Joseph Abboud, paired with $500 Bosca Italian wingtips.

There's a moment of pseudo-genuine connection between them as the two lock eyes ... but then they quickly revert to her "let's-get-back-to-business / no-nonsense-is-still-my-middle-name / we're-here-to-make-money" attitude, and his "let's-not-take-this-transformation-too-seriously / I'm-still-the-same-fun-loving-goofball / don't-let-the-fancy-duds-fool-ya" posture.

Then the music swells, the credits begin to roll and the audience exits the film assured that no matter what the obstacles, It Girl and Boy Foil are destined for a lifetime of fun, frolic and financial success!

Now, pass the Kleenex, please.

48

'I Believe in Miracles,
You Sexy Thang!'

Variations on this scene have only been filmed about ten *thousand* times. Yet Hollywood's top directors and leading actors never seem to flinch when the script calls for yet another re-enactment of a modern-day miracle never actually experienced by medical science.

Here's how the event unfolds in Movieland: Our hero — naturally — is engaged in an incredibly risky, extremely dangerous mission that involves facing lots and lots of shooting from various military assault weapons, high-powered rifles and numerous (too numerous to count) small-arms fire from an endless supply of bad guys.

After dodging about six or seven *hundred* rounds (a miracle in itself!), he finally gets nicked by a stray bullet, which hits him in the shoulder or in the fleshy part of the leg. If it's the latter, *fuhgedaboudit*; it's not even worth worrying about in subsequent scenes.

I mean, get real. A bullet wound to the leg of a movie hero is about as serious as a mosquito bite on the arm of someone in the Real World.

But if it's a classic "flesh wound" to the shoulder, then yes: The director has to make sure some blood-soaked clothing is visible for the next couple minutes of the movie.

However, despite the pain (and "Pain don't hurt!"), the loss of blood and the extensive damage to vital muscles and nerves, when the inevitable fistfight begins — after both hero and bad guy run out of ammo and simply toss their thousand-dollar weapons aside — why, the hero can throw punches with either fist, grapple hand-to-hand and otherwise finish off the villain in a vicious street brawl without once wincing in pain or failing to land a haymaker with his injured arm.

But that's not the best part. After taking care of the baddie, he's ready to sweep up his smokin' hot love interest and head off to the sack. If the nearly fatal gunshot wound is even mentioned again, it's in the context of "Oh, that little scratch? I'll get it looked at after we take care of some … unfinished business."

By the next morning — or whenever their 12 hours of nonstop lovemaking are concluded — the arm's all healed and the guy's as good as new.

Probably better.

47

'We Don't Need No
Stinkin' Warranty!'

Wouldn't you love to own one of the Hollywood vehicles that the typical hero or heroine uses to flee the cops / bad guys / killers-for-hire? You know, those unassuming, production-model look-a-likes they pilot on a suicidal escape attempt through crowded urban neighborhoods at speeds that would raise eyebrows among NASCAR drivers?

Of *course* you would!

Because then your little beater (or beat-up taxi) would suddenly transform into one of the most indestructible machines ever created by modern technology. Seriously, aircraft manufacturers should junk those flimsy black boxes they're currently using and switch to whatever material is used to manufacture these Movieland cars.

That's because "Like a Rock" isn't just a clever ad slogan, it's a factual description of the composition of the body, chassis and drive train of these getaway vehicles — assuming the rock we're talking about is hardened granite, that is.

How else to explain how one of these automobiles can survive a non-stop series of collisions that sends dozens of police cars or high-performance SUVs smashing into light poles and over cement barriers — when they're not going airborne at high speed and flipping into a triple sideways rollover a gold medal figure skater couldn't duplicate then bursting into a fireball worthy of a petroleum tank farm explosion upon impact?

By the way? That was a rhetorical question.

46

Wrong Place, Wrong Time, Right On!

In this all-too familiar clip, what might be called the Holy Grail of action scenes, some low-life sprints into the street in a desperate attempt to escape his pursuers, only to get clobbered by a speeding delivery truck and literally sailing through the air (in Super Slo-Mo, naturally) before smashing into – what are the odds? – a police cruiser that just happened to be driving by at that exact moment.

Which, of course, allows the director to pan from the bloody corpse impaled in the windshield to the exchange of shocked looks between the "old school" cop behind the wheel and his young hottie of a partner, then settle on a close-up of the coffee that got splashed onto the donuts they had sitting on the dashboard.

Right ... like that's the worst part of the outcome.

45

Cyborg Or Human: Who Can Tell?

There's a little known but universally applicable trick to determine whether the stone-faced assassin you're about to fight is a robot. It's just too bad that most Movieland actors never bother to read the memo from the studio (Subject: "Bot or Not?") before shooting the climactic confrontation scene.

We'll share the secret in a second, but first, let's answer the question: Why does it matter? Who cares if your opponent is a flesh-and-blood *Homo sapiens* (subspecies *Diabolicus*) or merely a cybernetic organism surrounded by living tissue?

Well, A-lister angling for that Oscar nod, it matters because you can't reason with robots. I mean, they can't be bargained with. They don't feel pity, or remorse, or fear, and they absolutely will not stop — *ever* — until you're dead!

So trying to talk a cyborg out of letting the girl go, while focusing on decapitating only you, ain't gonna cut it.

That said, here's how you quickly determine whether your cinematic foe is real or robotic:

When a human evildoer (although usually one with several bionic body parts) turns around after you brazenly call them out — typically with some truly original challenge like, "Hey, f**k face!" — they turn their head, revealing a malevolent smirk, then swivel around to face their opponent.

But when a robo-borg fresh off the assembly line is confronted with the same challenge, they turn their entire upper body first, *THEN* swivel their head.

It's a minor but ultimately crucial distinction, and it literally means the difference between life and death for the hero and his estranged girlfriend / supermodel partner / innocent tween-ager caught up in the confrontation.

Oh, wait. I stand corrected. The hero's not going to die no matter who (or what) he's facing.

But as a moviegoer, you can use this trick to determine the difference — and then share that revelation loudly and arrogantly with either the friends and family trying to watch the film in your living room, or with the entire theater audience, as the case may be.

44

❖—————◯—————❖

You Can't Bet Just Once

Directors, producers, documentarians — heck, freshman film studies students — never tire of including a gory and gratuitous bare-knuckle fight scene in virtually any film set in a time period somewhere, anywhere in the past.

To judge from the prevalence of these violent vignettes, fist fighting ranks right up there with working, eating and fornicating as activities that occupy most people's waking hours.

Here's how such scenes typically unfold:

First of all, it's always — *ALWAYS* — a huge mismatch. The good guy underdog / reforming-anti-hero / victim-turned-avenger is smaller / younger / less skilled, usually all three, versus their bigger, rougher, tougher opponent.

That means for the first several minutes of the contest they basically serve as a human punching bag, stopping numerous blows not by putting up any defense, or — god forbid — ducking the cascade of punches, any one of which would send the average human straight to the hospital, but instead by using their face to try to damage their opponent's hands.

Or so it seems.

Of course, if the fight is a "pay-per-view" contest there has to be a huge crowd surrounding the open field / barn floor / empty warehouse where the semi-legal battle is unfolding, and both contestants have to be stripped to the waist.

More importantly, all the extras in the scene are always pictured yelling nonstop as they wildly wave a wad of bills for some overweight tout to collect their bets, the odds on which seemingly change with virtually every punch as the brawl progresses.

But I have to ask: Are you allowed to continually change your bet every few seconds, depending on which way the fight's going? Can you do that at the track or during a football game? Because it sure would increase the chances of winning!

The other essential visual in such scenes is blood ... lots of it, freely flowing and typically accompanied by one (or both) of the fighters spitting out half a dozen teeth as the bloodbath proceeds.

Oh yeah: the director needs to frequently cut away to close-ups of the good guy's posse / crippled brother / estranged girlfriend who's had a change of heart, as they cringe in pain with the full-frontal assault that can be heard with a clarity it would be hard to duplicate if the fighters were wearing mikes.

No need to spell out the conclusion of these scripted brawls, because they never vary: The heroic good guy somehow manages to turn the tables on an opponent twice his size with a comeback that's not even close to plausible.

Then again, c'mon. There's nothing in these Movieland scenes that's remotely believable. Why should the happy ending suddenly pretend to be realistic?

You don't have to answer that.

43

I Can Fly, I Can Fly, I Can Fly!

Speaking of poetic license, in this ridiculous-but-let's-pretend-it's-plausible scenario, when directors need to pull off a "believable" escape sequence, all they need is a runaway tractor-trailer, a collapsed bridge over a bottomless canyon and enough suspension of belief that moviegoers will buy the depiction of a 10-ton vehicle flying through the air.

With the greatest of ease.

Here's how the scene unfolds in Movieland: A Bad-Guy-Who's-Really-Good and a Girl-Who's-Really-Good-When-She's-Bad have stolen a fully loaded 18-wheeler and are fleeing their pursuers.

Suddenly, they come to a bridge that's broken off in the middle — you know, like so many other bridges that have totally collapsed but there's no gates or fencing or warning signs, or even or a strip of plastic tape across the roadway. And yawning beneath them is what looks like the Grand Canyon.

What do they do?

What all movie heroes do: The guy floors it. The camera shows the speedometer hitting 70, 80, 90 miles an hour. Guy and girl start screaming. They hit the end of the broken bridge. And then suddenly the truck soars into the air with greater aerial loft than the Goodyear blimp, and after a flight the Wright brothers would have envied, they land safely and smoothly on the other side of the canyon.

Oh sure, they blow out a couple tires, and stuff's flying all around the cab, but other than that, they're good to go, and — surprisingly — the truck suffers no real damage upon slamming onto the other end of the roadway at nearly 100 miles an hour.

Now, here's how that scene would play out in the Real World: Same speeding truck. Same gutsy acceleration. Same boy-and-girl-screaming as they hit the end of the bridge. Then, in a matter of seconds, the truck plunges straight to the bottom of the canyon and is destroyed in a gigantic fireball.

Which, I'll grant you, doesn't really help move the plot along all that well.

42

Welcome to My Humble Coffeehouse

Used to be that roadside diners had a tradition called the bottomless cup of coffee. Although that's gone the way of the tabletop jukebox, Hollywood's well on the way toward reviving that particular perk.

That's because the houses where Movieland characters live are apparently connected to a full-service, 24-hour Starbucks right next door. No matter what time of day or night it is, the line, "Would you like some coffee?" is followed immediately by the matronly confidante / statuesque-but-stand-offish gal pal / still-superhot ex-love interest pouring out a couple steamin' cups of joe.

Of course, her buffed-out partner / platonic pal / hunky ex-lover never actually drinks any of the stuff during the pair's heart-to-heart, but who cares?

There's another fresh, full carafe all set to go for Take 2.

41

How Hard Can It Possibly Be?

Of all the fears and phobias with which Movieland characters must learn to cope, a perennial favorite of rom-com directors is one that wouldn't make most people's Top Two Hundred List of Things That I Fear:

"Learning to Dance."

While you might agree that bustin' out some slick moves on the dance floor at a hip new nightclub would indeed be a pressure-packed situation, that's not what we're talking about here.

No, this ubiquitous scene involves the estranged-but-still-emotionally connected tomboy daughter of a super-manly hero, or maybe one of his bumbling bros whose computer wizardry is matched only by his abject clumsiness around music, women and any conversation with the same — not to mention an apparent lack of coordination not normally found even in newborn babies.

You know: a left-brain nerd with two left feet.

But for all of the protestations about how unnerving the character's lifelong anxiety about dancing has apparently been, when the music starts to play, the "lesson" involves the kind of slow dance shuffling that *anyone can do without any practice at all!*

Seriously? We're supposed to believe that the character's debilitating angst over his or her absence of the choreography gene is all about not being able to stand there, arms around a partner, and then move six inches one way, then six inches the other way?

Then rinse and repeat?

Wow …

40

A Keyboard Wizard ... with Such a Supple Wrist

We've all witnessed this cinematic showdown innumerable times: As precious minutes fly by, there's only one — slightly whacko — computer "genius" with the sheer moxie to defeat an evil mastermind's lethal countdown to total planetary destruction.

But as the savant works at his computer, you can't help but ask: What the heck's with all that typing going on?

Even as the geek is offering a running commentary raving about how brilliant the bad guy's programming is — to the point he's practically achieving orgasm — he's banging out the equivalent of 120 words a minute, without ever once looking down at the keyboard, as he works feverishly to crack the super-secret firewall only a master-hacker / slacker like himself could hope to breach.

What, he never heard of a mouse? Or a touch screen? Or voice command? We're supposed to believe his hardware's so cutting edge he can match wits with an ultra-evil super-villain, but he has to manually type in innumerable lines of code just to enlarge an image on the screen? C'mon, really??

Yeah. Really.

39

Totally Shattered — and LOVING It!

When I build my next dream mansion, I plan to get all the windows and patios doors installed by Movieland Glass® Inc.

That way, should I accidentally trip and crash through the full-size French doors leading to my sprawling pool deck, or if a pack of hired thugs arrives to take me out because I double-crossed Mr. Big on a major drug deal and my only escape is diving head first through a second-story window, I won't have to worry about getting killed — or even getting cut — by the trauma of smashing through triple-thick panes of glass.

In fact, Movieland Glass can install car or truck windows that, should I need to escape my pimped-out SUV as it sinks to the bottom of the Hudson

River after careening off the GW Bridge while escaping some shadowy hitmen out to stop me from sharing those top-secret computer files I uncovered in my day job at the CIA, I can simply smash out the windshield with the palm of my hand and not worry about getting injured.

Believe me, this miracle glass is a worthwhile household improvement, and one you might want to consider asking your favorite diner / trendy bistro / neighborhood watering hole proprietor to install in those giant street-facing window frames — just in case you happen to get caught in the crossfire of a violent shootout or a full-scale bar brawl and have to exit the premises by taking a "shortcut" through said windows.

In such circumstances, after you crash through the glass, you wanna be able to hit the sidewalk in a nice, tight front roll, bounce up to your feet and start running — as opposed to having to fumble for your phone while you're lying in the gutter gushing blood and dialing 9-1-1 so an ambulance can transport you to the nearest emergency room where surgeons have to put in three or four hundred stitches to close up the multiple gashes on your face, arms, legs and torso.

I'm just sayin' ...

38

Chopper vs. Handgun: And the Winner Is?

Here's the scenario: A turbo-powered helicopter gunship is firing 50-caliber rounds from its front-mounted machine guns at somebody 20 feet below who's stumbling across an open field.

The guy on the run, in contrast, has only an old-fashioned revolver, with which he fires off a couple wild shots at the hovering chopper (without even looking, since he's busy "covering" his head to avoid the strafing). His aim is further complicated by the fact that there are billowing clouds of dust being kicked up, seeing as how the chopper is so close to the ground.

Question: What happens next?

In the Real World, the poor slob gets shredded worse than a bucket of coleslaw as a result of being hit by several dozen bullets, while the helicopter pilot simply elevates and zooms off after taking a couple seconds to confirm the kill.

In Movieland, however, not only does the guy manage to dodge a full 30 seconds of withering machine gun fire, but one of the bullets he randomly fires from his snub-nosed pistol miraculously hits the copter's rear rotor, immediately rendering it inoperable.

That causes the aircraft to lurch into an increasingly violent tailspin, from which, as the "experts" scripting such scenes know from their extensive aviation experience, it's utterly impossible to recover.

Within seconds, the helicopter nosedives into a building, or maybe into some high-voltage transmission towers, and explodes like it was carrying several tons of C-4.

The gun-toting actor — well, his reaction depends on whether he's playing a steel-jawed hero or a comic relief character. If it's the former, he merely smirks in grim satisfaction, and you can practically read his thoughts: The faster they fire, the sooner they go down in flames.

If he's a loveable loser, though, he'll first stop and stare at the sheer size and scale of the Hindenburg-like explosion, then look down at his revolver in shock and surprise.

Which is totally appropriate, *because a handgun can't shoot down an armored helicopter!*

C'mon, people. If it were that easy to take down a military combat chopper, then those Iraqi street fighters equipped with AK-47s mounted in the bed of a battered Toyota pickup should have been able to destroy the entire U.S. Air Force.

But I suppose even movie producers are entitled to a little "poetic license" once in a while, right?

37

The Storm (Ain't) a Comin'

We're conditioned to accept that the odds in Movieland are always stacked against the bad guys, that an evil antagonist's motley crew of henchman, whose on-screen half-life is measured in mere minutes, is eventually gonna get gutted, guillotined or otherwise dispatched in gruesome fashion by the star(s) of the show.

Come on! They're the *bad* guys, don't ya know?

However inept they might be at confronting, much less defeating the heroes, none of these nameless villains surpasses the futility of the endless parade of Storm Troopers in the space-epic series that cannot be named for copyright reasons but which rhymes with "Car Stores."

Although these losers are outfitted head to toe in what by all appearances is total body armor, just a single laser blast invariably drops them like a sack of rocks. And not just individually, but entire spaceships full of 'em.

It's beyond preposterous.

I mean, you're the ruler of a vast galactic empire. You have incredibly sophisticated technology to facilitate space travel. You have communications systems that operate without the usual constraints, such as the fact that even light beams are limited to only 186,000 miles per second. And you have weaponry that makes 21st century assault rifles look like plastic toddler toys.

But you choose to protect your seemingly invincible operation with a horde of faceless (literally) guards who collapse with the first volley from nothing more than hand-held pistols like they were sprayed with Goldfinger's invisible nerve gas?

Really?

Here's the underlying problem, though. Despite the fact that *EVERYTHING* about combat in the far-off future is unbelievably advanced, there seems to be one glaring deficiency: armor manufacturing technology in the 31st century seemingly never progressed past the stuff that Lancelot and friends were wearing back when "high tech" was a jousting lance that *didn't* shatter into a million splinters when striking an opponent's shield.

Storm Droopers would be better brand for these legions of white-suited guards who in the entire history of the film franchise have yet to dodge a bullet, actually win a firefight or even notice the good guy commandos hiding just a few feet away from wherever these clueless mercenaries are mindlessly marching.

The "fight scenes" with these guys gives new meaning to the phrase, "If I had a galactic cred for every Trooper I've wasted …"

36

The Swiss Family Armani

TV's a way worse offender, but even big-budget blockbusters about people lost at sea or out in space continue to stretch moviegoers' credibility.

That's because after surviving a near-death encounter with a howling blizzard / raging typhoon / exploding asteroid, the marooned travelers / shipwrecked survivors / stranded astronauts up on the screen only need one leisurely afternoon spent scrounging around their mountaintop forest / tropical island / alien planet and ... *presto!*

Next morning, they're outfitted in fashion-forward cutoffs for the guys, form-fitting fur togas for the ladies and highly functional footwear for the entire party made from slabs of some high-tech material that fits better than Birkenstocks.

Hey, maybe they discovered some synthetic rubber trees growing nearby. You never know.

Best of all, even in a remote wilderness or on an uninhabited planet, the characters skip right past the learning curve it took our Stone Age ancestors millennia to complete and go straight to 21st century technology when it comes to building a shelter, fashioning tools, starting fires, hunting animals or catching seafood — even though they're equipped with nothing more than some sharp rocks, a length of vine and a couple seashells.

All the activities that took humans eons to master only require Movieland heroes less than 24 hours to perfect.

And they look really sharp while doing it.

Well, you know what they say: You gotta look good to act good.

35

Timing in Life: It's the Only
Thing That Matters

From time to time, we all experience close calls (as opposed to Close Encounters): A near-miss fender-bender, a slip on an icy sidewalk that almost lands you on your butt (or worse), or maybe ducking underwater just before getting bashed by a seriously large wave while body surfing on vacation in Hawaii.

But those lucky breaks are nothing compared with the slew of narrow escapes even the supporting cast experiences in virtually every scene in every Roman numeral version of the Star Trek / Star Wars / sci-fi genre. For example:

- Seconds before the entire spaceship implodes, the lead actors manage to launch an escape pod and get away, despite a raging fireball that's already engulfed the entire command deck.

- Or moments before hideous aliens vaporize an entire search party, they all "beam up" back to the ship — minus one or two secondary characters who are likeable but expendable.

- Or an instant before the Death Ship's escape maw slams shut, the good guys somehow zip their space-going go-kart through an impossibly small opening — at warp speed, of course — while a whole fleet of enemy pursuit ships crashes into the now-closed exit hole.

No matter what the scenario, there's one essential element: The heroes have to be led by a super-cocky, risk-taking, no-room-for-rules personality. Man or woman — doesn't matter.

When it's time to hit "Go!" on the seemingly impossible task of dodging two dozen laser-firing attack vessels, or pushing a crippled ship's speed past any previously recorded limits, or maybe sneaking into enemy headquarters to take down the entire operation with only a furry alien and a talking robot for back-up, there's not only less than a nanosecond's hesitation, the hero / heroine actually *embraces* the suicidal mission with barely restrained glee.

Why? Because they've already signed a contract to appear in the next installment in the series, that's why.

34

The Lockup Lineup

Of all the stereotyping Hollywood's so fond of, nothing surpasses filmmakers' devotion to the utterly predictable casting that characterizes a prison movie.

You know those notes on location, backdrop and ambiance that screenwriters insert into the script to "set the stage" for the dialogue? Forget it.

You're shooting a prison pic? Notes aren't needed, because the entire cast and crew already know exactly how the set, the setting and the scenarios are going to be treated.

The prison itself is dark, decrepit and depressing, something straight out of the Spanish Inquisition. The warden is always cold, ruthlessly efficient and over-the-top creepy with his undisguised disdain for the human flotsam and jetsam behind bars that he makes sure are as miserable as possible.

Then there are the guards, who are mean-spirited,

testosterone-fueled sadists whose opinion of the inmates is lower than their own IQs, which barely hover above room temperature.

Speaking of inmates, they're divided demographically into several subsets, the most popular of which are these three:

1. *Shirtless Black Street Thugs*, who spend all their time in the yard lifting weights, shooting baskets and glaring at anyone who dares to wander within shouting distance of the bench press stand, b-ball hoop or outdoor bleachers where they congregate.

2. *Bandana-clad Latino Gangstas*, who spend every second on-screen mouthing threats to everyone else, calling each other "Essay" and fashioning shanks from pieces of melted cellophane.

3. *Tattooed White Skinheads*, who stick together like Siamese quints and whose hatred of anyone of color is exceeded only by their love of anything related to Hitler, Nazis or the Third Reich.

    After all, nothing says "white superiority" like a swastika tattooed in the middle of your forehead, right?

Just the process of slowly panning across each of these ethnic representatives of the dregs of humanity occupies a good 10 to 15 minutes of the movie.

Hell, throw in a couple shower-room stabbings, a racially motivated cafeteria brawl and a few close-ups of the zombie-like losers confined to "The Hole," and half your 90 minutes' run time is accounted for right off the bat!

33

'Look, Ma: I Can Walk and Talk!'

This filmmaking tactic (allegedly) became popular on the hit TV series "West Wing." Maybe so; wherever it originated, the approach quickly spread to the big-screen, and now it's commonplace to have actors walking straight at the camera while talking non-stop.

The sequence features two hotshot boy and girl lead characters who're heading somewhere apparently as far away as those airport concourses that require an automated tram to get there. Consequently, they're moving at a speed that would challenge Olympic racewalkers for a spot on the medal stand — even as they carry on a conversational sparring session with more back-and-forth than the Lincoln-Douglas debates.

Of course, there has to be an undercurrent of sexual tension even hotter than the pair's heated dialogue. But despite that distraction, each actor manages to fire off a dozen different *bon mots*, rebuttal points and dagger-like dissections of the other one's argument in less than the 30 seconds it takes them to arrive at … well, it really doesn't matter where they actually end up.

I mean, life's a journey, not a destination.

Am I right?

32

Summertime ... and the Parkin' Is Easy

Anyone who's spent more than 60 seconds driving around a congested, big-city neighborhood knows the frustration of attempting to park your car when the only options are "Screwed-by-the-Second" parking meters — and there's rarely any available — or forking over a Jackson (or two) for the "privilege" of leaving your vehicle in a dingy parking garage or at an even less attractive parking lot, both of which are typically staffed by guys you'd swear have mug shots on display at Post Offices nationwide.

But in Movieland, the lead actors never have to deal with that noise. When they pull up to a midtown office tower at rush hour, or that hotspot nightclub on a Friday evening, or a trendy *ristorante* at the height of lunch hour, gee — there's an empty space right in front that's so roomy they don't even have to parallel park to fit in their hopped-up SUV.

In fact, the spot's so choice, so unbelievably convenient that asking for one is officially excluded from the list of Make-A-Wish fantasies people can request.

What moviegoers don't see, however, are all the permits and payoffs to city officials, police captains and Streets & Sanitation bosses that it takes to secure even 20 feet of curb space for the half hour required to shoot a 10-second scene.

The price tag for that action makes big-city parking rates look like loose change in comparison.

31

Hangin' Out, Hangin' On

There's a universal principle embraced by virtually every director who ever had his/her name splashed on the screen at the beginning of the epic film they helmed. It might as well be a disclaimer attached to their title, and it goes like this:

"This is Movieland — not the Real World."

This principle exempts the director, as well as the entire cast and crew, from having to stay anywhere within a couple Zip Codes of reality as it's experienced by the audience soaking up their mega-blockbuster.

But there's one departure from the Real Word that is so egregious it can't be dismissed as mere "exaggeration," a momentary fling with a fantasy world we know doesn't exist — yet it shows up in what seems like every other Hollywood production to hit the market.

This scene features a hero or heroine who gets pushed over a bridge railing / shoved out of an airborne helicopter / knocked off a 100-foot construction crane.

Only they don't plunge to their death.

Instead, the hero / heroine manages to grab onto a steel I-beam / a landing gear brace / a swinging metal cable — with one hand, since the other one is either getting stomped on by the bad guys or is being used to pull out a 9-millimeter and fire back at the perps.

In some of the more outrageous scenes, the good guy or girl hangs on so long that, should you happen to be watching some straight-to-cable action / adventure classic, you could get up, hit the john, come back, grab a bag of chips, open a beer and settle back down … and the actor's *still* hanging onto a speeding chopper / swinging from a construction cable / rock climbing down the side of a skyscraper, *sans* ropes.

I defy any normal human being to hang onto anything with one hand for more than 10 seconds without serious strain on one's entire musculature. Even Olympic gymnasts are like, "Dude, I never do that in training. What, you think I wanna blow out my shoulder?"

Add in the imminent threat of instant death from a couple hundred feet in the air, should your grip slip even a little, and even 10 seconds would be a serious stretch.

But in Movieland? Even female detectives / pot-bellied sidekicks / plucky reporters-turned-crime fighters can pull off a one-handed hang-and-hold that would challenge an adult spider monkey.

It's as unrealistic as it's ubiquitous in Movieland, but it does make for an exciting 30-second clip that will someday show up at the Oscars when the now 90-year-old actor's wheeled onstage to accept his/her Lifetime Achievement Award.

And it will look just as ridiculous then as it did when the film was first released!

30

Whiskey River Don't Run Dry

There are three generally recognized signs that you're becoming an alcoholic:

1. Drinking before noon
2. Drinking alone
3. Drinking the whole bottle

Wait — let me re-phrase that last one: Killing an entire fifth of liquor isn't a sign of alcoholism, it's a sign you need to summon an ambulance to go get your stomach pumped.

Yet in every genre from lighthearted PG-13 comedies to dark character-study dramas to cheesy one-star cable pics about a lone wolf / tough guy / soldier of fortune on a bender, it's not at all uncommon to see Movieland characters sucking down enough booze in a single sitting to stagger a rhinoceros.

The signature shot in all such scenes is the long line-up of empty shot glasses sitting on the bar as the actor's best buddy / estranged spouse / former partner arrives to cut him off, drag him out of the bar or the party and force him to accept a cab ride home.

But guess what? The worst that happens in Movieland binges is that the drunk starts singing and clowning and rolling out really bad come-on lines to anyone of the opposite sex within earshot. Most times — especially with hardcore heroes — the whiskey river the actor's swimming in has about as much effect as you or me sniffing a stick of incense: A wrinkled nose, a sudden sneeze, maybe slurring a couple comeback lines. And that's about it.

I guess some people can handle an entire vat of Scotch better than others.

29

The Rules of the Road

You know how colleges require students to complete a number of prep courses before they're allowed to pursue studies in their major? Well, here are some of the "prerequisites" with which casting agents, directors and screenwriters need to demonstrate familiarity before Day One of shooting on the set can proceed:

- Actresses who have to fistfight hardened mercenaries / track down international smugglers / chase after F5 ("Finger of God") tornadoes must be properly attired: Tight slacks (or short-shorts), high-heeled boots and a-couple-sizes-too-small tank top, preferably one that's soaking wet.
- Both actresses and actors scheduled for scenes involving bare-knuckle brawls / prison yard

work details / iron-pumping health club workouts will be issued spray bottles of Body Sheen©, the leading man/lady's preferred product for creating that thin, glistening layer of moisture — as opposed to the rivers of sweat experienced by actual athletes during actual exertion.

- For storylines that call for extensive footage of an arrogant assault on a never-before-scaled mountain peak / a desperate trek across an Arctic wilderness / a week of survival in some post-apocalyptic frozen wasteland, the actors and actresses whose credits appear at the beginning of the movie must never, *ever* don scarfs, goggles, ski masks or any other cold-weather accessory that might interfere with the director's plans for shooting extreme close-ups during the film's romantic interludes.

Ridiculous, you say? Hey, I'm not the one making up the rules. I'm just the reporter here.

28

A Crappy Contractors' Convention

Most of us have experienced the bummer that results from hiring a cut-rate contractor. The shoddy work these hustlers specialize in leaves everyone they touch — either firsthand or vicariously — angry, upset and out-of-pocket even more dough than originally planned, because now someone else has to fix the mess they left behind.

You'd love to take it out of their hides — if you could ever track 'em down, that is.

Well, here's a good place to start looking: Hollywood.

That's because in virtually every Movieland script where the hotshot heroes / bumbling good guys / career criminals have to surreptitiously enter or exit a building — or any of the areas within — they always run up against a ventilator screen, a sewer pipe cover or an air duct panel that can either be effortlessly kicked out or simply lifted off with somebody's bare hands.

No tools needed! These (allegedly) secure panels, which supposedly are installed with screws, nuts and bolts, practically fly off the first time anyone nearby so much as sneezes.

Which can only mean one thing: The contractor decided to skip the part of the installation that called for attaching the panel to its framework with actual fasteners.

And the worst part? Those guys are getting paid like the actors!

27

First They Fight, Then They, um, You Know …

Here's an important tip for aspiring film directors out there: Nobody — but nobody — in Movieland meets somebody, gets to know them and then begins a relationship that smoothly progresses through compatibility, intimacy and ultimately, matrimony.

No way, no how.

After an initial surge of romantic interest, boy and girl must encounter a huge roadblock, a glaring *faux pas* or even an egregious betrayal. Got that? Movieland characters have to break up before they make up; fight each other before they [*expletive deleted*] each other.

So here are some suggestions for that "problem" they have to overcome:

- The guy gets caught flirting / hugging / smooching an ex-flame — only, "It's not what you think! Lemme explain!" (But of course she never does).
- Or the girl innocently agrees to accompany Mr. Hunky Bad Boy to a party — only to end up in a compromising situation when he makes an unwelcome move on her. Which is witnessed by boyfriend's buddies. Who report it to him *sans* context. Which spurs him to initiate a traumatic break-up for all the wrong reasons.
- Or the guy's roommate / girl's BFF spend the entire first half of the film pointing out the myriad incompatibilities between the two, until they both start to think that maybe this relationship won't work out after all.

Hey — what are friends for, right?

Anyway, after the requisite loud and angry argument over the misunderstandings outlined above — best staged in a very public place — the pair agree to end it all and just walk away. Only here's the kicker: *They're both miserable without the other one.*

Even though their interests are totally dissimilar, even though their backgrounds are completely incompatible, even though their social circles are night-and-day different, they soon realize they'll never experience another second of happiness their entire lives unless they hook up again with Mr. or Ms. "If-Loving-You-Is-Wrong, I-Don't-Wanna-Be" Right.

In the Real World, the couple calls it quits and moves on, wiser for the experience.

In Movieland, the orchestra's already cueing up the soaring theme music that will fill the theater when the pair finally throws themselves back into each other's arms — preferably during a torrential downpour — and pledges to never again argue or fight.

Then they kiss for what seems like half an hour, and then they … well, you know how that story ends.

26

You're Already Dead — You Just Don't Know It

Anytime a Movieland character hands over a precious artifact or keepsake — could be an antique brooch, a special ring or an heirloom watch; the possibilities are endless — it's always accompanied by an emotional speech linking the item to some piece of family or cultural history of supreme importance to the person handing over the bauble.

Sadly, although they're blithely unaware of their impending fate, whoever receives the talisman is already dead.

It's axiomatic: The doomed heroine / courageous-but-soon-to-be-deceased soldier / coming-of-age-young-son undergoing a rite of passage with the "Old Man" has mere minutes of running time left to live, before enduring a tragic death at the hands of whatever seriously despicable villains are teed up as targets for the audience to hate on.

Then, the battered talisman, which miraculously survived the fiery explosion / gruesome torture / cold-blooded execution the recipient endured, winds up back in the hands of the very person who handed it over.

Which is their cue to launch a fierce counterattack on the bad guys, fueled by righteous rage at the death of their beloved / betrothed / significant other.

And the key to driving home the anger that's driving the protagonist? A long, lingering close-up of the talisman as the avenger tightly clenches it in his/her fist.

Seemingly obvious, but mandatory nonetheless.

25

The Swiss Army Super Knife

Here's the scene: In the midst of a lonely, hardscrabble Western desert, with only some scraggly cactus and an occasional tumbleweed to relieve the brown-and-beige monotony of the forbidding landscape, a pair of Movieland protagonists gets caught up in a fierce gun battle with savage Indians / ruthless cavalrymen / bloodthirsty *banditos* hunting them down to snag the sacks of gold dust they're toting around.

But during the fight, the hero's partner takes a rifle shot to the chest, and collapses in the dust.

After a touching scene in which the stricken companion laughs off his imminent death with a throwaway line like, "Guess I won't be starting that cattle ranch I been dreamin' about, huh?" he silently succumbs (no unpleasant wailing permitted in Movieland death scenes).

So now his partner's gotta make sure he receives a proper burial.

Even though he was under attack from an overwhelmingly superior force just moments ago, he finds the time to make sure his fallen *compadre's* interred in a nice, well-constructed gravesite with a magnificent view of the valley below and topped with dozens of evenly sized boulders, among which is propped up a wooden cross hand-carved with the guy's name, his hometown, his date of birth, his date of death and some cornball slogan like, "A hero in life — A hero in death."

Funny, but I didn't notice any shovels, pickaxes or sledgehammers sticking out of the good guy's saddlebags. I guess he's just really, really skillful with that single-bladed Bowie knife strapped to his gun belt, a versatile implement that apparently doubles as an entrenching shovel / stone-cutting chisel / precision carving tool.

It's doubtful if Batman could come up with more effective implements from his utility belt to duplicate what one cowboy in the middle of nowhere can do with nothing more than a dull knife and, one would conclude, endless hours of time to dig, saw, chisel and carve.

24

Dumb, Dumber and Dumbest

This casting concept represents a Hollywood principle as immutable as Newton's Second Law of Thermodynamics: "Entropy increases over time" (*unlike* one's attention span during a boring movie).

Here then is Hollywood's Second Law of Character Dynamics: "Acting sets come in threes," and the higher up the food chain you go, the more dim-witted the actors become.

For instance: Take your typical high school comedy. First, there are the students. Although they're the day laborers of academia, a fair number are portrayed as shrewd, savvy and highly strategic as they plot to undermine the rules and rituals at good old Sunnydale High.

Movin' on up, there are the teachers, ostensibly endowed with substantial authority but almost always depicted as out of touch, out of the loop and fresh out of any ideas worth taking seriously by the pupils suffering through their sleep-inducing lectures.

Then, at the top, there's the principal, supposedly the boss of the school but always the last to know what's going on, the least-liked character in the cast and the most unlikely person to positively impact anyone, no matter how extensive their screen time.

Like I said: Dumb, dumber and dumbest.

Or take the business world — as seen through the lens of a Movieland camera, that is. At the bottom of the proverbial barrel are the secretaries and mailroom guys. They're barely making minimum wage, but they know everyone else's secrets, they control communications throughout the corporation and they have *way* better ideas than their big-bucks bosses.

Next, there's middle management: The supervisors, department heads and sales managers who should be clued in to what's going on, but are so bogged down in endless paperwork and useless meetings they have to be told what day of the week it is.

Then, at the top of the org chart sits the Big Cheese, the CEO, The Founder, who's so enveloped by a pack of butt-kissing brown-nosers that he or she has to struggle mightily with all the BS just to figure out which end is up.

And guess who eventually clues in the bigshot to

reality (after a scathing dress-down for his arrogance toward the "real people" doing the work)? The lowliest desk jockey in the building, because according to Hollywood's immutable laws, he's the smartest guy on the set.

23

'Scarface Ain't Got Nuthin' on Me!'

As the creative team sits around storyboarding the treatment of an action flick that's been green-lighted by the studio, there's one absolutely essential item at the top of the list of assets whoever's cast as the bad guy must possess: A viciously ugly facial scar.

Even better if it comes with a gruesome backstory involving something the good guy did to the villain years ago.

Like accidentally splashing hydrochloric acid in his face during a high school chemistry project gone wrong. Or taking out his eye with an inadvertent thumbing in a boxing exhibition during a stint in the Special Forces. Or badly gouging his forehead when a poorly tied knot slips while they're rock climbing up El Capitán.

Or it could just be the result of the bad guy's unredeemable cruelty, like getting half his face shredded off in his sleep with an electric cheese grater as revenge for a sex romp that got too rough for his abused and battered girlfriend.

(What a hardcore anti-hero's doing with an electric cheese grater in the kitchen of his Spartan digs is never properly explained, though).

In any case, no criminal gang leader is complete without a sordid résumé of death and destruction, a cold-blooded streak of pure, distilled sadism *and* a repulsive facial disfiguration that daily reminds the villain his primary purpose in life — when he's not robbing banks / shaking down rival drug gangs / extracting billions from the government to avoid deploying deadly nerve gas he stole from a secret military depot — is exacting revenge on his goodie-good guy antagonist.

(See, "Dick, Moby" and innumerable references to "My white whale!" Same deal).

However, the destruction he's planning for our Movieland hero has to come *after* he "makes him pay" for the humiliation of a lifetime watching people gag every time they catch a glimpse of what looks like raw hamburger yet is actually the "good side" of his profile.

Heck, it's making me sick just writing about it!

22

Armageddon Never Looked So Good

Although the previous two hours of cinematic spectacle have been a nonstop, wide-screen showcase in which a Good-Guy / Bad-Girl combo blows up half a dozen skyscrapers, firebombs an entire residential neighborhood, crushes innumerable cars and trucks beneath whatever earthmover, locomotive or other outrageous vehicle the director can dream up, smashes through block after block of sidewalk cafes and street vendors (all selling tall stacks of fruits and vegetables) during a futile high-speed chase, and for the capper, sinks a pair of luxury liners with cruise missiles they "borrowed" from the military, the final scene shows our heroes accepting hearty congrats from the President and / or some Army brass – who interrupt them while they're French kissing amidst the mud, blood and gore to *THANK THEM* for their help!

"Help," as in causing billions in property damage and putting several thousand people in the hospital!

Then, as literally hundreds of cops, firefighters and emergency personnel wander around randomly covering people in blankets, the movie ends with some lame throwaway line like, "Dis time, dey lurned a lesson." Or, "Let's go home. I had enough excitement for one day." Or, "Man, if this is Christmas, I can't wait for New Year's!"

Yeah. Me either.

21

'Protocol's for Pansies, Sir!'

Casting a rock-jawed renegade as the star of your next action-adventure flick? Here's a suggestion — no, make that a requirement: He's gotta be a go-his-own-way / alpha wolf / rules-are-for-rookies kind of stud. Someone with complete disdain for any sort of preparation that might actually help with the tough challenges he'll later face in the film.

You know, the kind of manly man whose occasional speaking lines consist solely of retorts like, "Training's overrated." Or, "Yeah, I read those rules somewhere. So?" Or, "Do you wanna go by the book, or do you wanna get this done?"

And he's always got a buddy / sidekick / platoon mate hanging around, someone who's nervous, fearful and paranoid, afraid to disobey even the spirit of the law. The male lead, in contrast, *lives* to break the rules. In fact, he never met a policy he couldn't violate, a regulation he couldn't ignore or a procedure he couldn't openly defy.

He's the anti-Manhattan Project: All guts, all "go," all gung ho. The only "manual" this guy's even aware of is the stick shift on the floor of his muscle car. And of course, his overactive, reptile brain-based decision-making severely dials up the danger, compounded by his perpetual seat-of-the-pants winging it in response to the not-inconsequential threats he has to confront.

In the end, though, the results are spectacularly successful.

While the best-laid plans of mice and men often go awry, our solo superstar's *worst*-laid plans ultimately save the day.

And the heroine.

And the planet.

And … roll the credits.

AND FINALLY:
THE TOP 20 ULTRA-PREDICTABLE,
TOTALLY IMPLAUSIBLE, YET SEEMINGLY
UBIQUITOUS MOVIE SCENES

The classic scenes and scenarios that have survived directors who've come and gone, studios that emerged, flourished and then got acquired by Disney and the relentless progress of high-tech that has impacted all of moviemaking.

Here they are for your viewing (or listening—this book now available in convenient audio form!) pleasure. The very best of the worst that Hollywood just can't back away from … slowly, now … slowly … and put the gun down!

No, no!! Don't ever put the gun down, Movieland hero — uh, unless of course you've got a surprise for the villain, that is

A scenario that's about as predictable as these final twenty scenes recreated below.

Enjoy.

20

Do You Believe in Miracles?

When it comes to CPR administered in Movieland, you can forget about the Red Cross admonition to pace the compressions to beat of the Bee Gees' hit song "Stayin' Alive."

Oh, no. When the stars of the show drag their nearly drowned lover / partner / family member up onto a deserted beach / floating wreckage / muddy riverbank just a few feet away from a fearsome crocodile, they start super-intense chest compressions to the beat of a universal snippet of dialogue:

"Don't … you … die … on … me … now!"

Miraculously, the heavy-handed CPR always seems to work — *if* the victim is an A-list actor / likeable character / under contract for the movie's Roman numeral sequel.

But the CPRing has to continue for interminable minutes, until all seems lost, until it's obvious the victim has no chance to survive, until the bystanders or fellow survivors are deep into the first three of the Seven Stages of Grief (shock, denial, and guilt).

Then and only then, can the victim revive, always with a classic move: Suddenly lurching up while spitting out what seems like a quart of water (clean, filtered H_2O, please) — and this is key — then almost immediately smiling / talking / passionately kissing the CPR-ist, whose job is done and can now shift into either the Robinson Crusoe role, should they be stranded on some desert island, or into a ninja commando, should they have barely escaped certain death at the hands of the movie's evildoers.

You think a near-death drowning incident might require more than six seconds to effect a full recovery?

Think again, my friend.

In Movieland, nearly dying after being submerged underwater for several minutes is more like a refreshing shower than a super-lucky escape from what would ordinarily be a certain fatality.

So if you ever find yourself floating face down in a river after being swept over a 100-foot waterfall, you'd better hope the cameras are rolling.

19

If at First You Can't Reach It ...

Okay, you're locked in hand-to-hand, life-and-death combat with a ruthless assassin / skilled mercenary / anonymous henchman who doesn't even have a nametag. Only one problem — other than the fact that you've been smashed in the face numerous times, kicked in the ribs, thrown bodily against a concrete wall, taken a knee to the nose and come within seconds of getting the life choked out of you with a steel chain, that is: The .45 automatic / serrated hunting knife / length of sharp-ended icicle you're reaching for is j-u-u-u-s-t a bit out of your reach.

Hard as you stretch out your arm, the weapon is millimeters away from your fingertips.

Or maybe you need to grab a flash drive containing a copy of the military's secret nuclear codes before the supervillain's hired thug snatches it and the countdown to Armageddon begins.

In either case, it's just a numbers game.

Of *course* you're not going to be able to reach what you desperately need the first time, or even the second time. But trust me: As the seconds tick off toward the mega-explosion that will destroy everything within three adjacent time zones, don't worry.

You're gonna finally snag that weapon, dispatch the bad guy in gruesome fashion, stop the countdown, disarm the bomb, save the planet and amazingly recover in mere moments from injuries that would take people in the Real World months of post-surgical rehab to even start the process of healing.

See, that's one of the perks of being a movie star. Not bad, eh?

18

The Amazin' Motel Maze

Although such construction doesn't exist in Nature, screenwriters and directors continue to be tempted by the plot twist of a motel room (always some decrepit fleapit) that comes equipped with a rear door.

C'mon! Who builds a second exit in the back of a $39-dollar-a-night dump? What, so the lowlifes who typically stay there can slip out without paying? Please.

Granted, a back door does allow the actors to make a wonderfully convenient escape as the drug lord's hit men are breaking down the front door, but I got news for Hollywood: They'll leave the light on for you, but they don't provide matching front-and-back exits.

17

Sweatin' to the Nightmares

Just like the rest of us, Movieland characters occasionally experience the trauma of a bad dream. Only theirs are incredibly well-choreographed, extremely dramatic and enhanced with CGI effects that are simply stunning.

Nothing like the mundane dreams the rest of us might experience, like showing up to work without your pants or straining to outrun a snarling German shepherd while seemingly mired in quicksand.

Oh, no. Cinematic dream sequences are either wild outtakes of earlier comic scenes re-filmed with the protagonists on steroids, or the culmination of the Worst Possible Outcome of however the bad guy villain, evil terrorist or paid-off gangster intends to snuff out the lead actor.

However, moments before machine guns erupt in a fusillade of bullets, or a demented wizard's monstrous creation bites off their entire torso, or the angry ex returns with a military-grade flamethrower to inflict revenge on her hapless former partner for his (alleged) cheating, lying and/or being unforgivably wimpy, the star of the show awakens with a rush, sitting bolt upright like they were just hit with high-voltage Taser — and most importantly — drenched in more sweat than an NBA center at crunch time in the 4th quarter.

Happens to the best of 'em, apparently on a regular basis.

If they happen to be under contract with a major movie studio for a series of rom-com or horror flick sequels, that is.

16

The Clueless Commander

Whether it's a civilian defense expert, one of the Army's top brass or the actual Chairman of the Joint Chiefs himself, when an evil super-villain seizes control of the military's ICBM launch codes / death-star satellite / ultra-poisonous nerve toxin, the decision-maker's entrance into the testosterone-drenched sit room is always preceded by a bellowed retort, "What the hell is going on here?"

Well, genius, what's going on is that the bad guy — a deranged ex-black ops specialist who formerly worked for the CIA / NSA / FBI and is well-known to everyone else in the room — is out to destroy the capital / the country / the entire constellation mere minutes from now.

(And don't you love that giant countdown timer visible on the dozens of JumboTron-sized screens broadcasting the villain's lengthy extortion speech, in which he demands some ungodly ransom to be transferred to a specific bank account? Which apparently can never be traced to actually locate him after his planned destruction is complete.)

Too bad the general / admiral / Cabinet secretary in charge is totally in the dark. That necessitates a lengthy briefing on the spot, wasting precious time, followed by a ridiculously impossible command: "I want this madman stopped. I don't care how you do it, just get it done!!"

Yeah, hotshot. If it were that easy, would you still be standing there sputtering and shouting at the horde of technicians already working feverishly to negate the threat?

Don't think so.

15

The Safe House Saga

As the action-adventure flick nears its climax, the hero-on-the-run pleads with his sidekick, "Just get me to a safe house I know about across town. We can't stay there, but at least I'll be able to pick up some gear and devise an escape plan so we can get the hell out of the city."

Hey, stud: Just askin'. If you're able to drive across town to a location that's so hot, so well-known to your adversaries that you can't stay there more than a few minutes, lest the killers locate you, bust through the door and fill you full of lead, why not just keep driving right on out of town?

Yeah ... didn't expect an answer.

14

Going Down ... or Just Going Away

Here's a predictable vignette that's a staple in plenty of cinematic productions, from low-budget action flicks to Hallmark Channel tear-jerkers to big-name, big-screen jewel-thief thrillers.

As the hero / heroine / villain steps into an elevator in the mega-skyscraper / super-modern office tower / swanky condo building, the doors slowly start to close, while the actor stands right in the middle of the car — nowhere near the actual panel with the floor buttons — and mouths some snarky put-down for which there's no comeback.

That's because the doors shut tight before anyone can answer.

All you get is a smug close-up as the doors are closing. It's Hollywood dogma: If an actor walks onto an elevator — no matter what the scenario — the director is contractually required to have them swivel around and face the camera, as it slowly zooms in for that lingering signature shot.

And while we're on the subject of elevators, take a good look around next time you're riding in one.

Notice how that easily accessible panel in the ceiling is perfect for popping out of place, pulling oneself up through the opening like an Olympic gymnast, replacing the panel and then hiding on top of the car, where the cables and pulleys that operate the elevator are located — all in the space of time it takes for the elevator to drop down a couple-three floors.

As a result, the drug cartel hitmen / S.W.A.T. team commandos / assault rifle-packing mercenaries in full body armor are reduced to scratching their heads when the doors re-open, wondering how the heck the occupants could have just disappeared.

And where did they go? Who could possibly figure out that mystery?

What? You say that virtually every elevator you've ever ridden in *doesn't* have a removeable ceiling panel easily reached by anyone less than seven feet tall? That it would be extremely difficult to hoist yourself up into a two-square-foot opening dressed in a business suit or a skirt and high heels? And that it would take several minutes, plus a step ladder and a mechanic's toolbox, to even attempt such a feat?

Well then. I guess you're not going to be cast as an extra in the next such Escape-From-the-Elevator scene, are you?

13

⟶⟶⟶───◦───⟵⟵⟵

The Abandoned Warehouse: Fully Loaded

Imagine the most run-down, graffiti-tattered urban wasteland you could possibly imagine. Who would have guessed that right in the middle of all that desolation there'd be a 50,000 square-foot, pimped-out warehouse equipped with full electrical and HVAC services, where a gang of evildoers can safely conduct their nefarious affairs?

Pretty much every screenwriter in the business, that's who.

Sweet as the set-up usually is, however, there's a big problem: Even though a swarm of several dozen bad boys is either shoveling slalom-sized mounds of coke into plastic bags on a factory-style assembly line, or else fine-tuning a command-and-control operation set to fire laser beams from an orbiting satellite, the masterminds calling the shots always forget to latch those old-fashioned dormer-style windows up on the roof.

Darn it!

As a result, the good guys can simply trail a suspicious black van right to the site, wait until the thugs inside get past the "secret entrance" — otherwise known as the front door — then clamber up onto the tin roof (which surprisingly doesn't alert anyone inside), force open one of those windows and not only scope out the entire operation exposed below but actually pick up on a conversation between Mr. Big and his No. 1 enforcer as they reveal crucial details about the time, location and personnel involved in the plot.

And the allegedly super-smart crooks inside never, ever glance up or notice the two guys right above them who are practically falling into the building as they strain to listen in.

If you're a career criminal, you gotta hate when that happens.

12

The Dinner Table Disaster

Whenever teens, tweens and parents share a Movieland household, you can be assured the characters fit neatly into time-honored Hollywood stereotypes:

A). The adults are obsessed workaholics who have so many meetings, late-night deadlines and out-of-town travel it's a wonder they manage to eat, sleep or bathe. Either that, or they're aging hippie types whose laid-back, *laissez-faire* attitude toward parenting, career progress or any semblance of family life borders on the pathological.

B). Likewise, the youngsters in the film are similarly typecast as the adolescent equivalent of those stock photos you see on websites featuring an Asian, a Caucasian and an African-American — all grinning in full kumbaya mode — only in this case, the diversity's represented by a super nerdy third-grade computer geek; a way-too-hot teen-age daughter who's more "mature" than most college co-eds; and a school's-for-suckers smoothie who at age 13 is already the mover and shaker of the entire family / school / neighborhood — usually all three.

Of course, the tension between the generations is so thick you need night-vision goggles to navigate through the household. And it all comes to a head one evening as Overcompensating SuperMom sets out a lavish spread that rivals a State Dinner. Or it might erupt as Culinary Challenged Single Dad botches yet another attempt at a mac-'n-cheese entrée that ends up the consistency of hardened epoxy.

Doesn't matter what's on the table, what's on the menu is *CONFLICT!* No Movieland family ever resolves its problems by talking — at least not during the first hour of the film. Instead, the characters resort to explosive outbursts, hair-trigger temper tantrums and plenty of flipped plates, smashed dishes and overturned glassware, plus most of the main course angrily deposited on the floor.

Which is the cue for the lumbering but loveable family mutt to amble over and start gulping down the pot roast or casserole that was so nicely positioned between a pair of lighted candles just a couple minutes ago.

It's all so warm and fuzzy, you can't help but ... *gag!*

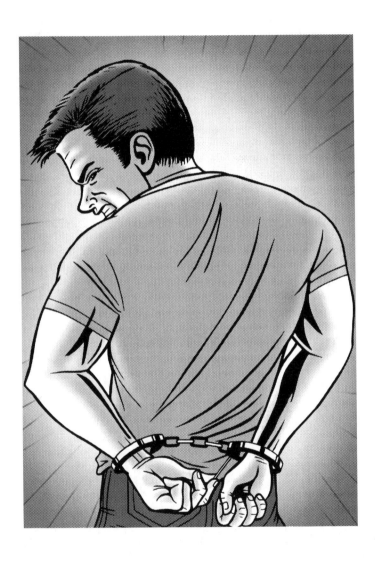

11

A-Pickin' and a-Grinnin'

Sometimes when you get a door key duplicated at your friendly neighborhood hardware store, even though it looks *exactly* the same as the original, it just won't turn the lock, no matter how hard you try.

Here's the solution, courtesy of Movieland's cadre of hardcore criminals and/or law enforcement personnel with "special skills:" Just get a length of wire, a broken bobby pin or even a piece of your own toenails *and pick the lock!*

It's not that hard, it rarely (if ever) fails and it only requires a couple seconds — less time, actually, than it would take to fish out your key ring, fumble around for the right key and turn that heavy-duty deadbolt the "conventional" way.

For example: A couple bad-guy *domestiques* handcuff you and your ex-supermodel-turned-PI partner to a giant steel I-beam, where you're supposed to remain trapped as the entire warehouse explodes in another minute or so. Good thing you managed to pull a nail out of your partner's boot heel so you can unlock the cuffs, sight unseen, from behind, seconds before the nuclear-scale blast goes off.

Or, maybe you need to break into a shady Mafioso's mansion to plant some bugs. The hard part is getting past a slew of overweight, brain-dead hit men in sharkskin suits standing guard on the lawn, in the driveway, looking out of windows and strolling across the porch.

The easy part is picking the lock on the steel-plated front doors that look like they were lifted off the set of Jurassic Park. For that, just insert paper clip, wiggle rapidly, open door, disable alarm, install bugs, exit premises. What could be easier?

Unfortunately, as Movieland security systems go all high-tech, lock picking is becoming a lost art. I mean, who's going to teach the next generation of hotshots how to open those giant doors at a secured airplane hangar with nothing more than the metal spring from inside a ballpoint pen?

It's something that keeps me up at night.

Behind locked bedroom doors.

10

Senile Security Inc.

Okay, I know the wages are low, the benefits non-existent and the shift schedule ... well, it generally sucks.

But why is it that when either the degenerate crooks or the renegade heroes need to crash the party at some super-secret government lab where they're developing a vaccine / virus (take your pick) that will save / destroy the world, all they have to do to bust into the supposedly ultra-secure site is smash their car through that flimsy wooden barricade and take down some creaky rent-a-cop who's so old his name badge reads "Pops" and so arthritic he couldn't restrain a newborn puppy?

C'mon! Why can't they afford one of those buffed-out bar bouncers? You know, the guys with no necks and biceps that are practically shredding the sleeves of their size-too-small muscle shirts. At least one of them could put up some resistance — before being annihilated with a semi-automatic, laser-sighted Uzi 9 millimeter with extended banana clip, that is.

And to top it off, instead of staying inside the booth, where he might have a chance to hit the alarm, Grampa Guard usually gimps right out to the car to peer inside, thus making it even easier for the smirking villain to pump a couple slugs straight into the geezer's pacemaker.

Ya hate it when that happens.

9

A Match Made in
~~Heaven~~ Hollywood

For an action flick, detective drama, cop show or any variation thereof, the formula for fleshing out the starring roles is as follows:

'*The Lead Actress.* She's young, she's athletic and she's swimsuit-model sexy — *of course!* During the day, she's leaner and meaner than Linda Hamilton doing chin-ups in Terminator II, but she goes all soft and feminine after the sun goes down.

On the job, she dresses professionally in her role as a vice detective, forensics expert or criminal investigator — which means skintight, hip-hugging slacks that leave little to the imagination, paired with a form-fitting, low-cut camisole that leaves nothing to the imagination. In other words, yeah: pretty much what you'd expect any police officer to be wearing when she arrives at a crime scene.

Naturally, her character's smart, savvy and sharp-tongued, not to mention more skillful than a samurai at fending off busloads of hunky young wanna-bes. She drives an imported sports convertible a hedge fund manager would have to think twice about leasing and her three-story condo with either beachfront or skyline views is right in line with the living arrangements any other 20-something working in Southern California as a public employee would expect to enjoy.

Oh yeah: If you're a male actor on the set, never, *ever* suggest she can't do something because of her gender. That'll get you a swift rebuke if you're a colleague, or an even swifter knee to the nuts if you're not.

The Lead Actor: He's *GQ* handsome and nicely buffed out, though not in an overly chiseled, slave-to-the-gym sort of way, but more with the rugged look of a stud who's climbed the mountain athletically and now doesn't have anything left to prove.

In fact, he has a veritable laundry list of "doesn'ts:"

- He doesn't bother shaving regularly — but his manly stubble never looks unkempt.
- He doesn't care about fashion — that's for insecure losers.

- He doesn't worry about rules — those are for the neutered drones filling up the background in his action scenes.
- Naturally, he doesn't work at a desk — his office is the mean streets outside.

And most importantly, he doesn't bother with any legal mumbo-jumbo, like checking some bad guy's alibi or reading him his Miranda rights.

His gal-pal partner's better looking, better dressed and gets better lines. But although the chemistry between the two mixes like Nitro and Glycerin (which, coincidentally, happens to be the working title of a new TNT cop show drama under development), in the end, the guy's basically a good-hearted goofball who handles a kindergarten class, a Golden Retriever or a hardened criminal with equal aplomb: Dish out some TLC and if that doesn't work, go to the stern silence / playful swat / lethal handstrike cards, respectively.

In other words, both girl and guy are pretty much like the rest of us — only with nicer clothes, faster cars, swankier digs, better grooming, more adventure, hotter sex and career paths straight out of a best-selling novel.

Other than that ... same as us.

8

'Mega-Morphosis' ...
in Under an Hour!

Some spectacular transformations regularly take place in Nature, such as the emergence of a beautiful butterfly from a slimy larval "thing" that just days earlier spun itself into a tight little cocoon.

But those biological miracles pale in comparison to the metamorphosis that takes place inside of an hour or so of running time in Movieland, as a previously bumbling, stumbling weakling turns into a death-defying, commando-class ninja capable of taking down a hijacked airliner / speeding passenger train / fortified jungle hideout.

All by their lonesome — with nothing more than some newfound courage, a bunch of weapons confiscated from the succession of bad guys they've snuffed out and more sheer determination than a roomful of Medal of Honor winners.

How does such an incredible change occur? Easy: Just take a ho-hum, risk-adverse, otherwise timid showgirl / lab rat / desk jockey, expose him or her to the threat of ruthless torture and/or gruesome death at the hands of contemptible villains, and then stand back as the actor quickly grows a titanium spine and develops an itchy trigger finger that allows him or her to annihilate scores of nameless henchman, thanks to the rapid acquisition the tactical skills normally found only among Black Ops commandos.

The transformation is simply stunning:

- *Before*: The unlikely hero couldn't even figure out which is the business end of a 9 mm pistol. *Afterwards*: He or she can whirl around at the sound of footsteps and put a single slug dead center into a bad guy's forehead before he's able to aim — much less fire — his weapon.
- *Before*: The hero had trouble lacing up a pair of combat boots. *Afterwards*: He or she can defuse a ticking time bomb with the skill of a surgeon and more coolness under pressure than 007.
- *Before*: The hero balked at merely witnessing other actors gun down the evildoers. *Afterwards*: He/she not only loses all inhibitions about

killing, the body count they individually pile up is so staggering moviegoers couldn't keep count even if they wanted to.

The only thing missing is the hearty laughter and high-fiving that breaks out at the conclusion of the film, as if the good guys just won the Super Bowl, even though their "success" came at the cost of dozens of dead bodies.

Oh, wait. All that inappropriate celebrating actually does take place, doesn't it?

7

'I'm Talking Tomaz, and I'm Going to Kill You!'

In Movieland, what do you suppose are the "fundamentals" a would-be, ultra-evil, Earth-destroying psychopath is required to possess?

Animal-like cunning? Unbridled avarice? A white-hot hatred of all humanity?

Sure, sure. But those are just table stakes. Price of admission. Résumé basics without which you don't even survive the casting call.

No, no — the one intangible that cinematic criminal geniuses absolutely must cultivate is a mouth that won't stop flapping. A big ol' yapper they just can't keep shut.

I mean, it's all well and good to be ruthlessly cruel, to be a poster boy for sociopathic sadism, or even to exhibit a warped brilliance that, had it been turned toward doing good, probably would have cured cancer or figured out a free, unlimited new source of energy.

But in Movieland, what separates ho-hum, another-day / another-disaster masterminds from the A-List of Bad Boy Bosses is the ability to deliver the equivalent of a UN General Assembly address — *after* they've defeated the good guy's heroic attack and now have him tied to a chair with three dozen coils of rope and surrounded by a pack of heavily armed thugs.

Instead of just hitting the button that launches nuclear Armageddon, or flipping the switch that rains down death on half a dozen world capitals from a commandeered satellite, oh no — our super-smart, super-eloquent villain first has to launch into a lengthy monologue detailing how and why he concocted his scheme, the backstory of his descent into a lifetime of evil and, of course, the grandiose plans he has to "enjoy life" after he annihilates the entire planet with some never-before-deployed weapons system.

In fact, the script for such speeches reads pretty much like one of those allocutions that criminals are required to make at trial before their guilty plea is accepted by the court.

But the endless droning allows the hero to acquire all the necessary info needed to foil the evil plot — just as soon as he saws through dock ropes the size of the mooring lines they use to secure ocean liners with that tiny sliver of broken glass he picked up during an all-out brawl with the two dozen henchmen it took to subdue him when he was captured.

By the time the big boss realizes he shoulda shut down the speechmaking like, 20 minutes ago, he's eating a knuckle sandwich that's a mere appetizer to the complete devastation of his secret lair as it self-destructs seconds after the good guy dives off a 100-foot cliff into the surf and cheats death once again.

It's probably the tenth time he's done so in this one film alone.

But hey — who's counting?

6

Calcutta Office Syndrome

You'd think that realism would be high on the agenda of any reputable director not in charge of a Scooby Doo animated "mystery" adventure.

But you'd be wrong.

In this classic rom-com scene, the embattled mailroom guy on the make / plucky ex-secretary determined to hit it big / brash imposter posing as a rival executive makes their nervous entrance to the executive suite in the office tower where the climactic scene is about to unfold.

Only it's less of an office and more like a beehive, or maybe one of those African termite mounds where thousands of insects are scurrying across every ridge, trail and tunnel in sight.

According to virtually every movie of this genre, the modern corporate headquarters is a throbbing hub of constant activity, with people swarming like drones through the hallways, exiting various conference rooms in groups and hustling about carrying stacks of paper, parcels and folders to some unknown but apparently time-sensitive destination.

Even the employees who actually remain at their desks are likewise turning, talking, typing — anything other than what most office workers actually do all day: Sit and stare at a computer screen while sucking down coffee and shoveling in snacks.

Uh, or so I've heard.

5

One Swipe, One Kill

I don't profess to be some sort of expert in sword fighting, but it seems like j-u-u-u-s-t a bit of an exaggeration when the hero and his little band of bros in a medieval adventure epic get attacked by an entire swarm of armored combatants intent on chopping off their heads ... and yet they somehow manage to dispatch all two dozen of them without breaking a sweat.

Best of all, it takes but a single thrust or strike to either permanently cripple or actually snuff out each attacker. In the two or three minutes of action, none of the defenders lays so much as a chain mail glove on the stars of the show, while their ranks get decimated faster than you can say "Is that sword sharpened?"

And there's always a craven king or some illegitimate usurper up in a tower nervously watching the slaughter down in the courtyard below, as the realization sinks in that despite the overwhelming superiority in numbers, his days as a ruler, not to mention his time on Earth, is about to come to an abrupt end.

Thanks to the efforts of a mere handful of warriors equipped with nothing more than ordinary swords and, one presumes, unquenchable rage coupled with the stamina of a professional triathlete as they wipe out an entire castle-full of otherwise battle-hardened mercenaries.

And when they finally confront the cowardly bad guy, the hero and his pals inexplicably appear with their faces all nicked up (?). I mean, I could understand that look if they'd been trying to hack off their manly beards with an ax blade or something.

But how in the heck do you suffer facial scratches when you're fighting with broadswords? Seriously?

The bad guys are lying in veritable stacks of gutted and decapitated corpses, while the good guys look like they cut themselves shaving.

But whom am I to question history?

4

Spare the Whip, Spoil the Slave

In virtually every sword-and-sandal saga, whether in a big-screen epic or in some egregiously gory miniseries, it doesn't matter whether it's savage barbarians / implacable Conquistadors / or ruthless centurions, one slow pan is sure to occupy several minutes of run time: a long line of manacled slaves staggering as they haul wagons along a dusty pathway, or a group of aging, near-skeletons chained to the oars on a galley ship — all being maniacally whipped by brutal overseers for the slightest deviation from their assigned task.

It never occurs to the slave masters that if they eased up on the beatings, those emaciated prisoners might actually get more done — especially since their work assignments include such projects as hauling 20-ton blocks of limestone up the side of a pyramid or rowing a wooden warship across the Mediterranean Sea in the middle of a hurricane.

Apparently, if we're to believe the way directors imagine such scenes, the goal of the conquerors who ravaged the ancient world was to kill off as many slaves as possible with nonstop whipping, I guess to save on the high cost of that single bowl of gruel they were fed once a day.

On a good day.

If they were lucky.

Too bad they didn't have corporate accountants back in 4000 B.C., because that slave-management system wouldn't have passed even a rudimentary cost-benefit analysis.

3

When Time Stands Still

They say that if you want to slow down the way each day seems to whiz by, just start exercising intensely. That 60 seconds of jumping jacks will quickly start to feel like it's lasting for an eternity.

Here's another way to accomplish the same goal, courtesy of the intellectual giants running Hollywood's major studios. Just do what movie stars do: pack a string of events, activities and a romantic rendezvous (or even an outright hook-up) into your day — no, make that your morning — that is more time-consuming than what most people could squeeze into a three-week vacation.

How is that possible, you ask? Well, for one, Movieland characters don't work — not in the sense the rest of humanity has to do, that is. Oh sure, they show up at the office or on a job site, but they don't have to spend hours creating spreadsheets, attending meetings or wasting time doing something as mundane as filing paperwork or unloading a truck.

Your 9-to-5 would feel much more productive, not to mention a helluva lot more exciting, if you could spend it wooing some smokin' hot honey, hunting down a gang of evil drug dealers or cracking a computer code to defuse a terrorist threat to nuke New York City and environs.

Before lunch.

In 10 minutes of run time.

2

Lighting the Eternal Flame

Hey, hunky Hollywood heroes and/or alluring heroines: Do you find yourself stuck in a pitch-black cave, but you need to somehow find the right exit tunnel? (What? You didn't know that all Movieland caves have an entrance *and* an exit? Wake up, Captain Clueless! It's called Cinematic Geology. Look into it).

Or maybe you got trapped deep in the labyrinth of an Egyptian pyramid while trying to find some ancient gold-encrusted totem that will impart magical powers, which you will shortly be in dire need of, because even though you're deep inside a 6,000-year-old stone structure smack in the middle of a bone-dry desert, it's crawling with hundreds of fully grown, super-aggressive snakes.

Or maybe you found yourself transported back to Roman times, and you're running through the catacombs to escape a legion of soldiers (who, no matter what the occasion, are always dressed in those standard-issue helmet-with-headdress, shiny-metal-breastplate-and-pleated-male-skirt-and-sandals combo) stomping in lockstep along the stone corridors.

In any case, you need illumination, right?

So just fire up a Movieland Inc. Perpetual Torch™. Whether made of rags soaked in some vaguely flammable fluid, or just a bunch of dry grass wrapped around a stick, these torches ignite effortlessly — no matches needed!

Not only can just one or two of 'em light up an entire 50-foot high burial chamber or the full length of a winding underground corridor with nice, even lighting suitable for motion picture filming, they can withstand wind, rain or swarms of bats without even flickering — and they come in mighty handy for repelling the attack of a giant cobra / enraged grizzly / pack of rabid wolves.

You think the Olympic Torch that carries a flame from Mount Olympus in Greece all the way to whatever city's bribed the International Olympic Committee for the privilege of going billions of dollars in debt to stage the Games is impressive? The torch that ignites a cauldron of flame burning over the Olympic stadium for a fortnight?

Big deal. A fortnight's only two weeks.

Movieland torches just keep on burning for as many takes as the director decides to shoot.

Which leads to the obvious question: What the heck are they running on? Atomic energy? C'mon, seriously. I defy anyone to fashion a torch out of a stick, a rag and whatever accelerant you choose — lighter fluid, jet fuel, napalm — and keep it going for more than a couple minutes.

Won't happen. Can't happen. Never has happened.

But in Movieland ... *no problemo!*

Word to the wise: Don't leave home (or the set) without 'em.

1

Do I Have to Kill You?

This universally staged scene is often the opener of a Movieland action saga, preferably a Roman Numeral sequel, featuring a conflicted, reluctantly heroic character. He/she possesses deadly fighting skills but hates having to use them on clueless mortals engaged in something as banal as carjacking.

Which is typically accompanied by the ruthless beating of a hapless motorist with a tire iron and / or capping his ass with a clip-full of hollow-point 9 mm rounds.

Sometimes, the star of the show in this cinematic genre is a truly gifted superhero who, if they weren't so world-weary they usually can't be bothered, could simply crush, smash or roast with some sort of laser vision the entire gang of low-information bad guys — who never, *ever* heed the hero's warning to cease and desist with their over-the-top criminal activity.

Or he/she could just be another straight-off-the-cybernetic-assembly-line avenger, an ice-in-the-veins, killing's-what-I-do, ultra-ruthless ex-commando-type who lives by only one rule: There are no rules.

In either case, the movie typically opens with a classic piece of action staging. The good guy/gal is reading a newspaper on a park bench, sipping a beer at a bar, or maybe riding quietly on a city bus, minding his/her own business while swimming in why-bother depression.

But within mere moments of screen time — before the movie even finishes running the opening credits — a bunch of loudmouth, low-life losers appears and starts harassing some helpless female, shaking down a wimpy businessman for his wallet and watch or stupidly trying to steal the tires off the hero's car — *while he's dozing in the front seat!*

You know what's coming, and it's so predictable you're practically shouting at the screen, "Just run away, you idiots!"

But they never do.

Instead, the hero's low-key warning, delivered in a tired monotone, only serves to fire up the gang members, who start taunting and threatening our solo superstar, as they (cleverly, so they suppose) surround him in a circle from which it's impossible to escape.

Ya'll can script it from there, with the only variable being how many guys actually get killed — either by getting shot with their own weapons, having their necks snapped like dried twigs or getting their heads smashed through the nearest windshield — versus those merely left with cracked skulls, severed limbs or missing internal organs.

But the one key ingredient is that the galactically stupid villains never figure out that they're only in the scene to wind up the hero who's listed at the top of the credits — you know, the actor who'll be bouncing up onto the stage in a couple months to pick up an Academy Award for Best Performance in a Starring Role.

Well, okay … maybe not an Oscar. Maybe a Golden Globe Award. No? Perhaps an American Film Institute Award? What, no? A New York Film Critics Award? No?? A Screen Actors Guild Award? C'mon!

What? Oh, yeah … a People's Choice printed certificate.

Congratulations. ☐

Other Books by Dan Murphy

In addition to ***The Hollywood H.I.P.* List***, Dan Murphy has authored previously published books, and is working on several upcoming titles. His other published works include:

- **"The Meat of the Matter,"** a collection of essays on food production, nutrition science and health and wellness.
- **"The Post-COVID-19 Survival Guide,"** a simple yet effective plan for families to manage the disruptions in schedules and lifestyles created by the coronavirus pandemic; co-authored with hypnotherapist Paulette Deckers.
- **"The 100 G.O.A.T. Sports Nicknames,"** the ultimate compilation of the most memorable, the most creative and the most beloved nicknames connected with the superstars, also-rans and wanna-bes of the sporting world.

All those titles are available wherever fine books are sold online.

Upcoming titles include:

- **"The Olympic 100: The Top 10 Olympians from the Top 10 Medal-Winning Countries,"** a collection of profiles of the prominent athletes from around the world who are celebrated as their country's most accomplished medal winners (publication date: July 23, 2021).
- **"The Mount Rushmore of All Sports,"** an illustrated collection of 100 all-time great athletes, coaches and managers who belong on a mythical Mount Rushmore

as one of the four most important people in their sports (publication date: October 11, 2021).

- **"1951,"** a deep dive into what was arguably one of the most pivotal years in American sports, at once a preview of the revolution created by television and sports marketing, as well as what are now recognized as a series of watershed moments involving many of the true legends of the sporting world (publication date: December 10, 2021).

Printed in the United States
by Baker & Taylor Publisher Services